THE

VESUVIUS

BRIBE

M. WILSON ATHEY

First eBook edition, January 7, 2023
Paperback edition, January 20, 2023
Hardback edition January 22, 2023

Hollylane Publishing

DEDICATION

In memory of S/Sgt Albert Francis Wilson, my father, and all the people he treasured: the Atheys, the Carrolls, the Malotts and the McDonalds. He loved us all.

And, Linda Sue Wilson Carroll, my sister and staunchest supporter. Without her, this book would never have seen the light of day. She died within sight of the finish line.

Table of Contents

PROLOGUE

San Sebastiano al Vesuvio, Italy
19 March 1944

Standartenführer Werner Lang sat stoically in the cab of a stolen US Army truck as it crept slowly through the streets of San Sebastiano. The place resembled a glowing chapter out of Dante's *Inferno*. Flashes of light from the erupting mountain allowed them to see the chaos the fleeing Italians had left behind. The streets were lined with abandoned furniture and suitcases. He could see some forgotten rocking chair sitting drunkenly on one side as the truck brushed past.

The guide who was driving the truck was obviously going by instinct, since headlights were useless. Thick masses of hot ash obscured the scene, accompanied by roars from the belching volcano; shaking earth; and the rank smell of sulphur. All in all, not a good night for this project, Lang thought.

He gave a mental shrug and decided that only the Italians would think it was a good idea to build a town on the side of an active volcano – one that erupted with alarming frequency. The Americans weren't much smarter, he mused, since they'd built an airbase at nearby Poggiomarino, from whence they'd stolen this truck. He conceded that the

Germans hadn't shone in the intelligence department either when they'd planned this operation. So, idiots all. And, it looked like he might be the biggest idiot as he peered through the darkness, searching for an old church and a quick exit back to Berlin.

Dressed as an American Army colonel, he had completed his disguise by dyeing his golden hair a dull brown. His hooded eyes were a cold amber shade. Two deep indentations ran from his nose to his down-turned mouth, evidence of the constant scowl he wore. Patience was not his strong suit.

He was jammed into the front seat between the door and Obersturmführer Karl Hesse, who was looking rather green in the intermittent flickers of light. The younger man occasionally plucked at the captain's bars on his American uniform – one that would mean an instant death sentence if they were caught by the real Americans. However, he knew better than to begin idle conversation with his colonel.

The Italian driver hadn't said anything for the past 10 kilometers, during which time he'd smoked three of the cigarettes Lang had given him. It had taken them 60 endless minutes to get this far.

The air quality made breathing uncomfortable and the door handle was digging into his side as he braced to keep from falling on the floor with every pothole. In spite of this, his situation was infinitely better than those poor bastards in the back with the cargo. The tarp over the rear was being decimated by the globs of simmering ash, and it offered little protection from the chunks of exploding rock that pinged off every surface. Fortunately, the cargo was sealed in metal containers.

That cargo was the reason he had been selected to lead this unbelievable fool's errand. However, in his opinion, fool's errand and Adolph Hitler were beginning to be more and more synonymous these days. A sentiment, he thought, that would also get him shot very quickly if ever uttered.

The Führer had decided that this trip was one that had to be made. It didn't matter that the area was crawling with angry Allied forces. He wanted Lang to be there; no questions and no objections allowed. Although, from the looks of things, it didn't appear that San Sebastiano would be *there* much longer. He hoped he wouldn't either and that his future was brighter than this town's.

He should put the blame, though, where it was due – that spineless blowhard, Benito Mussolini. He'd stomped his way through Italy for 30 years while becoming something of a hero to a rising young Adolph Hitler. When they'd decided to make Italy and Germany the 'Axis' of the new Europe they planned to build, he was all bombast and pomposity.

When the Allies finally talked King Emmanuel and his council into getting rid of him, Mussolini had called on the Führer to rescue him. Hitler had risked a crack SS unit to get him out of jail in the Italian mountains. The two met last September at Lake Campo where a tired, ill Mussolini begged Hitler to give him sanctuary in Germany.

The Führer, for all his admiration of Il Duce, wasn't having any of that. He still needed those two million Italian soldiers in the field to keep the Allies from landing at Salerno.

He'd set Mussolini up again as a puppet in northern Italy with German minders who ran the show and kept the war going. Mussolini had insisted Hitler make it worth his while. He'd named his price and Hitler agreed. The cargo they carried was quite simply a bribe – granted a very large bribe – but a bribe nonetheless. It was intended to keep Mussolini pacified and cooperative.

They still had the Americans pinned down at Anzio and Monte Cassino, but it was only a matter of time before they broke free. When they did, they'd overrun the German and Italian forces on their march to Rome. Italian soldiers were already throwing down their arms, shedding uniforms and running for home.

This brought his thoughts back to his current situation – the Führer's secret pact with Mussolini. Part of the inducement to keep Il Duce in the war had been the promise – the bribe – of a share of the looted treasure the Germans had been gathering from the conquered areas of Europe. Mussolini had chosen mostly great Italian masterpieces – Michelangelo, Caravaggio, Botticelli – as well as the majority of the jewels and gem-encrusted object d'art from the Rothschild collections. Those baubles resided in the small steel box that sat between his feet – along with a letter. Lang hadn't read it yet. The box was locked, even from his eyes. He had a feeling that letter might be more valuable than the rest of the cargo.

Lang couldn't imagine how Mussolini thought he was going to turn that well-known cargo into liquid assets, but he wanted it sent and sent now.

Maybe he thought the cargo Lang was taking to San Sebastiano would save him. Maybe if he was seen to be a hero, returning great Italian art to Italy, the authorities might let him retire in peace. Maybe he just wanted a pile of valuables ready for a quick getaway. Didn't Mussolini understand that his people hated him so much they would never let him live, let alone retire or escape?

Lang had been safely ensconced in Berlin, helping Hitler keep track of his various ideas for the new museum at Linz, when the order came that he was needed to oversee this operation. In a way, it was a compliment from Hitler, who thought Lang was the only one who could be trusted with this project. As he grabbed the door handle on the latest swerve to avoid a burning boulder – the damned rocks were getting bigger – he decided it was an honor he could have done without. He already had the Iron Cross; Hitler could keep the oak leaf clusters.

With one more savage smash on the engine's hood by a cannonball-sized rock, the volcano recaptured Lang's attention. It hadn't been this bad when they'd started two days ago. He and his team were transported by submarine to a small fishing village near Portici. The waters along the coast were teeming with Allied ships, but the U-boat commander had done this run many times.

A quick exit in a rubber boat had allowed them to arrive on shore at the same time a huge explosion from the volcano had claimed everyone's attention. That diversion helped them gain entrance to a waiting fishing shed. There they found his second-in-command, Lt. Karl Hesse, and his cannisters that had sailed in from Paris.

They'd spent the following day looking at maps and waiting for darkness, although that came early due to the volcano's discharge of ash. There were a few of Mussolini's Blackshirt fascists in the neighborhood who were infuriated by the Allied bombing that had badly damaged nearby Naples. They'd been helpful in procuring the truck; the false orders that would pass inspection; and a driver who knew the area intimately. If challenged, Lang and Hesse were both fluent in American English. So far, they hadn't needed that language, but it didn't do to leave things to chance.

Lang and company had started out the next night, assisted by the terrible visibility as they grew closer to San Sebastiano. The town was located on the northern slope of Vesuvius and had developed a fertile grape growing industry. Ironically, past eruptions by Vesuvius had covered the slope with the volcanic ash that grapes loved. It would be a good number of years, though, before grapes grew again on these slopes.

Suddenly their driver said, "C'è la Chiesa."

Lang's limited Italian, along with the driver's pointing finger alerted him to their arrival at the pride of the town, the San Sebastiano Martire church, dedicated to the patron saint, Saint Stephen.

As they lurched to a shuddering stop in front of the imposing front doors, Lang could see the falling rock and ash smearing the once-pristine cream stone exterior. Dirty paint, he thought, would be the least of its problems quite soon. He opened the passenger door to find the sergeant and his enlisted men already had the tailgate down and were shifting the cargo. They were as anxious as he was to be out of the ash that was quickly covering their faces and crawling down their necks.

"Let's see what we've got here," he said to Hesse as they both hurried up the stairs toward the shelter of the church. They found the front doors blocked by rubble. Their boots protected them somewhat from the heat of the embers as they kicked away enough to pry open one door.

"Gruber," Lang yelled to the sergeant. "I want to be in and out of here in 30 minutes."

He knew that was unrealistic, but the sight of Mt. Vesuvius limned against the sky by the glow of its infant lava flows was an excellent spur to their efforts. Before long, those infants would grow to be very large.

Willing hands and shoulders soon had the venerable church's door thrust back and propped open with a convenient needlepoint kneeler. Lang, closely followed by Hesse, strode down the center aisle, using powerful flashlights to penetrate the inky blackness. The lingering scent of incense was being overborne by the sulphuric fumes they had let in so abruptly.

They passed six side altars on their trip down the aisle, three on each side. Their guide had told them that the beloved statute of St. Stephen had been processed out of the church days ago when the evacuation orders began to be enforced.

The church silver had, no doubt, gone with it. However, they weren't here to take anything, which in itself was unusual, but to leave something. As he approached the main altar, he played his flashlight over the marble flooring obscured by the altar stone.

He was looking for something that might not be there – a thought he couldn't allow himself to believe after all this effort. He didn't know how Mussolini knew about this church or the fact that it was supposed to have a long-forgotten crypt beneath the main altar. Mussolini had an antipathy toward the Catholic Church. His mother, however, had been a devoted daughter of Rome, so she had sent her troublesome son to a religious boarding school.

Were hidden crypts a topic of conversation among boys late at night? Who knew? Local informants had checked that something seemed to be under the altar, but no effort had been made to open it. They didn't want to alert officials to their interest in it.

"Ah, there it is," he pointed out after sweeping aside dust and ash with his boot. "You can just make out the crack running from here to there." Using sweeping gestures, he showed the team where to look. Five soldiers and the driver moved forward to begin the heavy work of shoving aside an altar that hadn't budged in decades.

When they'd finished, they attempted to force pry bars into the barely-visible seam in the marble flooring.

"Careful," Lang warned. "We don't want any damage that would alert people this has been opened."

They finally got one end up and made short work of the rest of the long-closed stone. They balanced it against the altar they'd just moved so it would be easier to close when they left. Stale air wafted its way up from the gaping dark hole.

"Get some light down there," Lang directed one of his team. The man dropped two battery lanterns down at arm's length as he sprawled over the pit.

Roughly cut stairs were dimly illuminated at the end where Lang stood. Very little else was visible in the echoing space, but he didn't need to see very much. The stairs looked passable and that was all he cared about.

"Go bring in the cannisters," he told Gruber. The sergeant and his men trooped back to the truck to return carrying large metal cannisters, one each. The five men negotiated the stairs one at a time as Karl Hesse stood at the bottom of the flight holding the lights to guide them.

"You don't need to put them too far from the stairs," Lang said. "Just set them down wherever you can find a space. The other occupants down there aren't going to complain about the clutter."

In half an hour, the 20 cannisters had all been stowed between two ancient tombs. Gruber was halfway up the stairs with the others following when Lang said, "Just stay right there, Gruber." He then leaned over the edge to hand the sergeant the box he'd brought in himself.

"Lay this on one of the tombs," he directed. Catching Gruber's eye, he added, "And finish the job."

Gruber nodded his understanding. Setting the metal box on the closest tomb, he pulled his side pistol and turned. The four enlisted men were so stunned by this betrayal that they had no time to run. Moments later, all that was left were echoes of gunfire and some plaster dust stirred by the movement of falling bodies.

Before he could climb the stairs again, Gruber looked up and was shocked to see Lang pointing his Luger pistol at him.

"Sorry, Gruber," Lang said. "Der Führer said no witnesses."

With that, he fired the last shot. He lifted his eyes to meet Hesse's; then he lifted a brow.

"The orders were explicit; no witnesses. If you're wondering if I'm going to shoot you, the answer is - no. You are a fellow SS officer. You follow orders; your loyalty is dedicated to the Führer, right?" he said.

Hesse was shocked, but he quickly agreed. He'd known about the 'no witness order', but he assumed it was aimed at Italian civilians, not German soldiers. After all, Sergeant Gruber had left America to come to Germany when the war began. There was no more dedicated soldier of the Fatherland.

"Where has our friendly guide gotten to?" Lang asked Hesse.

"He's in the truck," Hesse answered.

"Well, let's see if we can lower this stone without him. Then we can get out of here. You can take care of him once he gets us back to Portici," Lang directed.

He gestured to Hesse and they wrestled the crypt stone back in place. Moving the altar was easier this time, and it slid into position without protest.

Back in the truck, Lang relaxed slightly. It was done. Whether the plan worked was not his concern. Now they had to hope their luck held as they made their way back to the coast. The Führer would be pleased. The bribe had been paid and there would be no loose tongues to talk about it.

Lang wondered if Mussolini would have time to get to the church for his promised loot before the political situation – or the mountain – blew up. However, that wasn't his problem.

Karl Hesse, glancing to his right, thought he saw Lang smile.

"Is something wrong?" he ventured. Lang never smiled.

"Do you not think it ironic, Karl, that the German Army has spent the past five years taking great art works out of Italy and sending them to Germany; and now we are going to all this trouble to sneak Italian paintings from German museums back into Italy?" Lang inquired.

CHAPTER 1

Jack

Poggiomarino, Italy
April, 1945

"Hey, Jack, wait up," yelled the American officer as he ran across the tarmac, recently home to the 340th Bomb Group.

Jack Evans, sometime archeologist and currently a captain in Uncle Sam's Army forces, pulled up to wait. Puffing up to him, Captain Ted Sanders pounded his back and said, "Man, it's good to see a familiar face. Where did you spring from? Do you know where we're headed from here?"

Jack laughed and shook Ted's hand. "Good to know that the officers in this man's army are still in the dark about what's going on. Gives a guy a feeling of continuity."

"Go ahead and laugh," Ted countered, "but I've been here for two days and no one seems to know when I'm shipping out or where. We may be winding down this war, but I'm not sure everyone's on board yet. And this base is sort of the back of beyond. It's still recuperating from the punishment it took when Mt. Vesuvius erupted all over it last year."

They both looked quickly at the looming mountain two miles away. It seemed quiet enough now.

Ted continued, "They had a bunch of planes destroyed and lost a lot of equipment. And, as you can see, there's still volcanic ash a foot deep in places. A couple of local villages got hit really hard."

"Yes," Jack said. "I could see a lot of the damage from the air as we were circling the field. As to what's going to happen next, I guess we're making it up as we go along. I know things are crazy at Ike's headquarters as our troops push the Germans back across the Rhine. It's slow going because the Germans know there's no welcome waiting for them back in Berlin.

"Then there's what happened with Mussolini. I suppose you heard they caught him trying to cross the border into Switzerland last month and this time they did more than arrest him. They tried his whole entourage in one day and executed them the next. The Italians may be slow about making war but they're hell on handing out justice."

Ted grinned, then fell into step beside Jack as they continued toward the mess tent. "I need something to eat," Jack said. "I haven't had anything since last night when I got picked up in France and ferried down here. This seems like a strange place for you Monuments Men to be sent, most of the action for your section is in France and Germany right now. I'm here as a favor to someone, but what are you doing here?"

Ted was part of a group of men who had been hurriedly assembled for their expert knowledge. They were military men, but first and foremost they were members of the Monuments, Fine Arts, and Archives section (MFAA). They were specialists in the art treasures of Europe – both finding and returning them.

"Well, there are several estates around here that belonged to the old Italian aristocracy where Hitler's merry band plundered everything from the art on the walls to the chicken coops. We're still not sure what happened to all the people. I've been assigned to look at a dozen villas and see if I can find any answers," Ted explained.

Jack knew the MFAA had covered areas all over Europe since the beginning of 1944. Much of what the Germans hadn't destroyed had been damaged by Allied bombing. Their big challenge now would be acting as a 'lost and found' department for European treasures, as civilians began to come to them to retrieve their stolen property.

"And, we still need to be in Italy to deal with our troops – officers and enlisted men. One of our biggest problems is keeping our own soldiers from picking up stray artworks and sending them home to friends and family. We've had to use the white tape that warns soldiers of unexploded mines to keep discoveries from being pilfered. They don't see anything wrong with taking home a souvenir or two." Ted added.

They found a table and a couple of battered-looking folding chairs and set them up in the shade of a green tent.

"Guess you can't blame them," Jack replied. "It's been a long, bloody war and everyone just wants to go home with something to show for what they've been through. And there are God-awful piles of this stuff laying around in caves and cellars, thanks to the German's hoarding and hiding."

They had both been updated on the recent discovery of hundreds of caves and mines that stored Nazi caches. In a copper mine in Westphalia, the Allies had encountered paintings by Rembrandt, Van Gogh, and Reuben. An original score of Beethoven's Sixth Symphony was also among the items found there.

A week later, the Merkers salt mine was opened and they found millions of Reichsmarks in gold bars as well as art from more than a dozen German state museums. Yesterday, just before his plane left, Jack had heard that Patton's Third Army had found a salt mine in Austria housing more than 6,500 paintings destined for Hitler's private museum in Linz. There was also stolen Italian art from Göring's personal collection. So, Italy was still of interest to the Monuments Men.

"I was on the transport plane with a guy from Harvard who was headed to Austria to help with emptying that mine and shipping the contents to Munich. They think it'll take two months just to get it all moved. Right now, they are using the Munich Central Collecting Point as a staging area, so I guess a lot of you will end up there to sort things out and try to find the rightful owners," Jack said.

They found a couple of dented metal cups and helped themselves to one of the endless pots of bitter black coffee. Ted took a sip, grimaced at the bite of the mixture, and got as comfortable as he could in the wobbly wooden chair. "You think that's where I'll be sent next?" he inquired.

"I don't know, but I'm guessing a few of you will be. After all, you're not a big group and the job of finding and identifying all these works, then locating where they belong, seems pretty overwhelming. You won't finish it in less than 10 years, you mark my words," Jack said.

"Why did they send you here?" Ted inquired.

"Well, you know art's not really my strongest area of expertise. My field is really Intelligence. However, with my background in architecture and archeology, they tapped me to do a favor for the base commander. Seems that one of the villages has a 16th century church that didn't fare well during the eruption.

"The local priest wants help deciding what they should do. Of course, that depends on how badly it's damaged and whether it's of any real historic value. With so many churches and monuments in need of repair all over Europe, this one is pretty small potatoes. But the priest is persistent and one of Ike's staff asked me for help," Jack said.

"What's the name of the village?" Ted asked.

"San Sebastiano al Vesuvio. Apparently, the residents are now part of the homeless problem caused by the eruption.

They've had a rough time, with the bombing, occupation, rationing and such. They sure didn't need a kick in the ass from Mother Nature," Jack said.

They were finishing their coffee when an Army pilot who'd just landed strolled in looking for a place to kill time.

"Mike," Ted called. "Come join us." The lanky red-haired pilot ambled over with his coffee and sat down on another shaky chair.

"Jack, this is Mike Kelly from New Jersey. Mike, Jack Evans from Connecticut," Ted said, making the necessary introductions. They sat down and settled back for a bull session.

"Hey, Ted, what's happening here today? I just got in," the tired Irish-American asked.

"Jack just arrived, too. I'm beginning to feel like the Welcome Wagon for the base," Ted said. "We're all still waiting for assignments. I'm off, eventually, to help the MFAA guys with their projects in Germany; finally put my college major in Fine Arts to use. Jack's going to visit a church that the volcano flattened to see what he can do before he's reassigned. What's your story? More hurry up and wait?"

"I'm not sure. I've got to see the base commander. I've been ferrying people in and out of here for the past three weeks, mostly from England. I don't know if that's what I'll do going forward. At least there aren't as many German planes still active in the area. That doesn't mean things are quiet," he said, pulling a battered cigarette case out of his pocket.

It opened to reveal a good supply of Camel cigarettes and a slightly dog-eared photograph of a young woman.

"Hey, pretty girl," Jack said, noticing the attractive smile staring up at him. "Your wife?"

"No," Mike grinned. "My twin sister. She's trying to decide whether to finish school at Wellesley or do 'something meaningful' with her life. Whatever that is."

"Probably means she wants to help out with the war like her twin has been. It isn't easy to stay at home while those you love are in danger," Jack said from personal experience.

"Kate is not renowned for staying in the background, that's for sure. But I'm glad she's been thousands of miles away from this hell. You a Yale man?" Kelly asked, pointing at Jack's class ring.

Jack was surprised at the question, but knew the surmise was obvious since Ted had said he was from Connecticut.

"No, this is Dad's ring. Actually, I went to Oxford. I wanted to get as far away from home as possible. The result of being an only child of a protective, widowed mother. I'll probably be headed toward Yale for postgrad though. You a Rutgers guy?" he asked

Mike shook his head. "I live in Princeton, so that's where I was studying. The Ivy League's been taking it on the chin recently. You guys hear about Joe Kennedy? He was in my squadron. Elliot Roosevelt's our commanding officer."

"Yeah, I heard just before I left England," Jack said. "Really tough about that plane he flew blowing up like that. Scuttlebutt was that it had an experimental bomb of some sort on board and it went off too soon."

Mike said, "That's what Roosevelt reported. He was behind them in a Mosquito; supposed to take pictures of the whole thing. But he was too close to Joe when it went up, so his plane got hit with debris and some of the crew was injured. Just a big foul up from the get-go."

All three were quiet for a moment, then Jack said, "When I was in boarding school, Joe and his brother Jack, along with some of the Rockefellers and a couple of Vanderbilt grandsons used to compete in regattas. Then we all ended up over here, with some in the Army and some in the Navy. The four Roosevelt boys are all over here, too, not just Elliott. Funny the way things turned out – definitely not what we expected."

Ted listened as Jack and Mike tossed off the names of the East Coast elite as if their names had been Smith or Jones. If Mike had gone to Princeton, Ted thought, then he probably knew some of the same men Jack did.

He, however, had had to scrape his way through Ohio State on a scholarship. Yet here they were, all in the same boat thanks to a German corporal who thought he was smarter than all of the Ivy League boys.

"What do you plan to do after this is over?" Ted asked, taking the conversation in a different direction. It was, however, a question on the minds of most soldiers in that long-anticipated spring of 1945. They all knew that once the peace treaty was signed, those who had been there the longest would get their tickets punched for a quick trip home.

"I'll be staying on for a while to help with interrogations. There's going to be a lot of payback for this war. Many of the leading Germans are going to go on trial, so our department is going to be really busy for a while.

"Maybe I can do a bit of digging on my down-time. Pompeii and Herculaneum have been ongoing, but I think there's still more to do there. Later, I might drift on down toward Sorrento and Capri to the sites of some of the old emperor's palaces. There's still lots of work there.

"Then I'll go home, maybe finish graduate school and try to live like a normal person for a while. I know my family would be glad to have me around New England for a change. My mother has been holding down the fort since my dad died," Jack said.

Jack had been in the Army for two years, but before that, he'd gotten his degree in languages and the classics from Oxford. It had been a long time since he'd lived at home. He'd spent some time touring Europe before the war, and had decided on archeology as a career.

That hadn't set well with his family, since he was the sole heir to a manufacturing and real estate conglomerate of world-wide importance. They wanted him around to lead the corporation after his education was finished, and they had certainly fought his entering the Army.

His flat-feet had kept him out for a while, but he'd found a way around that little problem. After all, he topped six feet, was sound of health other than the feet, and had a higher IQ than most of the generals.

He wanted a piece of the war and, because he had old friends in the right places, a solution had been found. He'd joined the civilian OAS who'd then loaned him to the Army Intelligence office to question captured enemy prisoners using his multi-lingual skills. He'd eventually been given an Army rank to make things official. Then he was transferred to Europe as the need for experts in French and German had become critical.

"Sounds like a good plan," Ted said, bringing Jack's thoughts back to their conversation. "Maybe when you get home, you'll find a cute young thing whose been waiting just for you to tie the knot."

Jack shook his head at that. "No, not me. I've got years of field work ahead of me and I don't plan on getting tied down with a wife and kids."

He stood, stretched and looked around. "I guess I'd better report in and see about getting transport to San Sebastiano so I can get this ball rolling. The sooner I'm finished here, the sooner I can help with the really big projects. See you later."

Turning to Mike Kelly with a twinkle in his blue eyes, he said, "Hey, if I'm ever in Princeton, I may look up your twin, Kate, just to see how you are, you know?" Kelly laughed and threw him a quick salute.

With that, Jack turned and asked a private who was clearing the tables for directions to the HQ. There he found the base commander just concluding a meeting with his staff.

"Hello, Evans. Glad you could come help us out on this," Colonel Dryden said, offering a quick salute.

"Glad to be of help, Colonel," Jack said. "Headquarters is a busy place right now, but I was told this was important. How do I find this priest? Father Tucci, is it?"

"Yes, he's a great old guy who's been the only priest in this little town for 45 years. He's really proud of his church, although I can't find anything particularly historic about it other than its age. And let's face it, in Italy, a 300-year-old church isn't all that rare," Dryden said.

"You're right there, sir," Jack agreed. "They've got structures that pre-date the birth of Christianity, so 300 years is relatively young. I think that year coincides with one the last times Vesuvius erupted so severely. The volcano must have taken out whatever was standing then, so they had to build this church. However, if it was in the town square, it's no doubt everyone's pride and joy."

Dryden called to his aide, "Stevens, call the motor pool and ask for a Jeep and driver for the captain."

Turning back, he said, "If you need anything else while you're here, just let Major Stevens know and we'll do everything we can to assist," the colonel said. Then he threw Jack a hurried salute and returned to his office.

In only five minutes, a dusty Jeep with a khaki-clad infantryman behind the wheel came to a quick stop beside Jack. He had noticed the jeep making its careful way around the potholes in the airstrip apron. A young sergeant with several stripes on his sleeve hopped out. He snapped a quick salute.

"Sergeant Albert Wilson, sir. I've been assigned as your driver for as long as you need me," he volunteered.

"Captain Jack Evans, sergeant. Glad to have you with me. Were you here when all this happened?" Jack asked, waving his hand at the dilapidated condition of their surroundings.

"No, sir," he replied. "I was a staff sergeant with two machine gun platoons who followed General Patton across Europe. But now that things are winding down, I've been assigned here temporarily. The rest of my unit is up in Czechoslovakia doing occupation duty, but I'm part of a mixed choir performing around Europe. This is my assignment when we're not singing."

Jack knew that anyone who'd ramrodded a machine gun unit through Europe, especially with Blood and Guts Patton, was not only tough, but lucky. The attrition rate for the sergeants was unbelievably high.

"Good for you, Sergeant. Are you appearing anywhere around here this week?" he asked.

"Not for another two weeks, sir, which is why I'm out here instead of in Naples where the next concert is scheduled. I'm glad, though. I've never been to Italy before and while it's not exactly looking its best right around here, it's still wonderful. I've had a chance to get over to the coast, too, and as a Missouri farm boy, I'm really amazed by the ocean. I wasn't that impressed when we waded ashore in Normandy last year, but this water is bluer and warmer."

Jack laughed as he threw a leg over the jeep's passenger seat and settled back. "Do you know where we're going? San Sebastiano al Vesuvio?" he asked.

"Well, yes, generally speaking. I've been here about five months," Wilson answered. "The roads between here and there have pretty much disappeared, and so have the sign markers. But I've made a couple of trips that direction, and if you keep aiming for the mountain, you can't miss it," he said confidently.

"You know," Jack said. "I've been told 'you can't miss it' so many times, I'm beginning to think I'm directionally impaired. What with the German shelling, the American bombing, and the devastation of the volcano; I think you can miss just about anything in Italy. At least I have."

Wilson gave an amused chuckle and depressed the clutch. "Let's go see, sir," he said.

As they bumped along the so-called road, Jack continued. "While this church we're going to see wasn't hit by one of our bombs, Mother Nature gave it a pretty good wallop. We'll have to see if there's anything we can do," Jack said. "You know, be good neighbors; help them dig out."

The sergeant grimaced at that term. Jack could see that Sergeant Wilson probably wouldn't feel that neighborly if it included digging anything. Most of the infantry had dug enough holes to last a lifetime as they'd fought their way across Europe, foxhole by foxhole.

They proceeded in silence for a while as Wilson expertly guided the Jeep around potholes and broken pavement. Occasionally, Jack would ask a question about a deserted farm or destroyed building, but mostly he just looked and was amazed by the still evident reminders of the eruption.

The volcano looming over them had quieted now, but it still looked dangerous. Jack had heard that more than 100 people had been killed and whole areas, like San Sebastiano, were destroyed by flying rock and lava flows.

"Five months, huh? So, have you heard any details about the eruption," Jack said.

"Yes sir, a lot of the guys who lived through it are still around. They sure like to talk about it. It all started about the middle of March last year. They say as the days went by, the eruptions grew louder and flames shot high in the air against the night sky. It seemed like the whole top of the mountain was burning."

He stopped at a crossroads to negotiate a sharp turn, then resumed. "This went on for two or three days. Then, early one morning, all hell broke loose. Black stones, some as big as footballs, starting falling from the sky. Soon all the tents were in tatters and everything inside was being destroyed. By this time everyone was wearing steel helmets and heavy sheepskin jackets for protection from the falling ash.

"Finally, about noon, it was decided to evacuate all personnel. They headed in convoy down toward Salerno. Kept getting lost because there was no visibility. They all said it was a damned long trip."

Jack sat in silence, picturing the convoy as it fled from the raging mountain. "I imagine it was like being in combat, with no way to fight back," he offered.

"Yeah, you're right. When it was safe to come back, they found 88 of the B-25 Mitchell planes were a total loss. The next night, Axis Sally dedicated her program to the 'survivors' of the 340th Bomb Group. No one was really hurt, but it was a mess. They moved cinders that were two-feet deep with snowplows to get the tarmac ready for flights and by April 15, they were back in business," Wilson concluded.

"Looks like they are doing land-office business," Jack said. "My plane from Paris had to circle for a while so two others could get out of the way. It's worse than Idlewild in New York."

Wilson just grinned and then pointed. "That's San Sebastiano, sir. The church is near the center of town. You're going to have to walk and climb from here. The streets are still impassable."

"Thanks Sergeant," Jack said as he eased out of the Jeep, pointing at a lone pine tree. "Park over there by that tree and I'll be back as soon as I can. It depends on how easy it is for me to find Father Tucci."

"I'll be right here, sir. You shouldn't have any trouble finding him. He was told yesterday that you would be here today. I'll bet he's looking for you," Wilson said as he pulled away, a *Stars and Stripes* newspaper already in his hand.

Jack looked around the village as he maneuvered his way through the broken streets. A few hardy souls had returned to pick up the pieces and one house that seemed in better repair than most sported a pot of geraniums on the windowsill. Wilson's prediction proved correct when he was hailed a few minutes later by a diminutive figure in a long black robe.

"Signore, buongiorno," he said. "La sono Capitano Evans?"

"Yes, Father," Jack replied in flawless Italian, a legacy of his Oxford studies and one of the things that had made him so valuable to the Allies. "I am here to see if we can be of any assistance in regard to your church."

"I am so grateful, my son," the priest said. "I don't know what you will find, but I pray to the Heavenly Father that it will help the people of this town. Please, come this way."

Jack followed the small man as he picked his way through the rubble to the sad-looking structure he'd come to see. It had a large central dome, much like a basilica, but on a smaller scale. One end had a tower and the opposite end housed the entrance, with the outer wall and doors still standing. There were no side walls.

Lava was piled several feet thick around the base. Left alone, time and Mother Nature would eventually turn it into a solid wall entombing the church.

Though it had not been around during the Crusades, it had lived through the Renaissance. It had stood against the volcano for three centuries, but it was evident to Jack that the mountain might have finally won.

As a kindness to Father Tucci, Jack climbed over piles of rubble as he circled the perimeter of the building, testing areas here and there for stability.

"Father, I'm afraid there's some serious structural damage here. Because of the piles of lava, I can't see the base to any great extent. It will certainly need to be rebuilt if it is ever to open again, and some of it may have to come down just to rebuild it.

"Your people may decide they would rather spend their efforts and money on a newer church that could be more resilient during the volcano's future earthquakes. I'm sorry," Jack said with a hand on the priest's shoulder.

"I was greatly afraid of this, my son, but I appreciate your coming to look," Father Tucci said. "It will be a while before all my people come home. Some may never come back. We shall see what happens."

Jack paused, then came to a decision. "What I will do, Father, is come back when the Army is finished with me. If some of the rubble has been cleared by then, I'll do an analysis of what needs to be done and help find crews to repair it.

"And I think I know a guy who is going to set up a foundation in the US to help restore some of the damage we've caused here in Europe. I'll bet we can find some money to help with rebuilding the church. It might take me a year to get back, but I won't forget you, I promise."

"That, my son, would be a miracle for us," said Father Tucci, obviously thrilled by Jack's offer. "I will look forward to that day. For now, go with God."

He finished up his blessing with the Sign of the Cross, and Jack moved back toward the Jeep. He spared one quick look over his shoulder for the church. He wasn't sure why he'd suddenly invented his foundation to help rebuild Father Tucci's church, but developing a charitable arm for the Evans Corporation seemed like an idea that had been simmering in the back of his mind for some time.

All the devastation he'd been looking at for the past two years was certainly going to need money to rebuild. His family's corporation had made money working for the government during the war. They'd built the weapons to fight it. Now it was time to spend some of it on projects he could choose. For now, it was back to the base and then the first plane out for Paris. He had a lot of work ahead of him.

CHAPTER 2

Kate

New Haven, CT
May, 1975

Kate Evans slid the last of her cosmetics into a plastic bag, sealed it and tucked it in the side pocket of her carry-on. After years of playing gypsy with her archeologist husband, Jack Evans, she'd learned to pack lightly, if nothing else. It had only taken a bottle of hand lotion leaking all over her best suede pumps to teach her.

A plain gold wedding band and a serviceable watch with a leather strap were her only jewelry. She was leaving her five-carat engagement ring and Cartier watch behind.

The canvas bag landed on the floor next to her old Hartmann Skymate suitcase just as Hugh, her butler and general factotum entered the room. Butler seemed like such a misnomer for the greying man who came into her life when she married into the Evans family.

She'd been a bit intimidated by him back in 1949, but now he was her right hand. He had helped her set up homes for her family in a dozen places around the world, and had kept the ship running smoothly at home when she was away. She couldn't picture life without him, but he was definitely approaching retirement age.

"Miss Elizabeth called over from the main house a few moments ago, ma'am," he said. Kate had long ago given up trying to break him of the habit of addressing her so formally.

"She will be here in 15 minutes to drive you into the city. If you've completed your packing, I'll put your luggage in the front hall," he offered. With that he hefted the battered bags, and preceded her down the hall to wait for her daughter.

Kate had dressed conservatively in camel cashmere trousers, a cream silk blouse and brown walking heels. Now she rummaged through her brown leather shoulder bag to make sure her frequently-stamped passport, traveler's checks and identification were in the zippered compartment.

She wouldn't need her keys, and they went into a tray on the hall table. They were quickly joined by two tubes of lipstick and a coin purse loaded with change. It was definitely time to lighten the load.

"Hugh," she said as she pulled out a sheet of paper. "I've made a list of where I can be reached while I'm gone. I've worked with Ivy, my secretary, so she knows how to reach me. But I think it's important you know where I am as well. I'll start out in Rome, but I have no idea where this trip is going to take me. If I end up missing, like Michael, you can have the police start at the hotel," she said jokingly.

"I've been in touch with my company directors, so they shouldn't need anything unless there's a world crisis somewhere. In that case, I'll get back to you as soon as I can find a phone. I'm going to let Jeff Brown, my deputy, worry about the Evans Corporation for a few days," she concluded.

"I'll make sure your business associates don't bother you unless it truly is an emergency," Hugh assured her. "I am glad I'll be able to track your movements if necessary. I wish someone else was going with you on this odyssey," he concluded.

"I know you'll worry," she said, "but I promise to be careful and I do have our offices in Rome and Paris that I can turn to, if necessary."

She took a last look at the painting of her husband on the living room wall. His cornflower-blue eyes always returned her gaze. On their first date, she'd looked into those eyes and he'd winked at her. That did it. She'd fallen in love with him on the spot. He'd been dead for five years now, and the pain was not as sharp when she thought of him. They'd had 22 glorious years and produced a beautiful set of twins. A grandchild was on the way, so the future looked bright. But she missed him.

They had consciously avoided becoming the stereotypical privileged couple who meet, marry and lead frivolous lives. Jack's life had been shaped by war and the carnage that accompanied it. After that experience, he'd tried to use his resources to add to museum collections, both large and small.

He didn't do it for the accolades, since most of the donating was done anonymously. He hoped the beauty of the shared exhibits might help calm the souls of a few potential warriors. Unrealistic? Probably, but untold thousands had toured the museums he'd filled with paintings and sculpture; as well as the cultural artifacts from at his sites. He had allotted nearly $75 million dollars to the cause over a 20-year span.

For a long time, she'd had her hands full with the challenges their lives threw at them. They had split their time between summer digs and winter business. Jack's family corporation would have been consumed all their time if he'd let it. Fortunately, his mother had still been in charge of things in their early years.

They had been a well-matched team. She had equal say in the decisions made at every turn. They chose sites together. They shared their interest in the museums and the charities that would receive their gifts. She had even begun her own career as a photojournalist before tragedy struck. The world they'd shared was shattered by a senseless auto accident.

She'd stepped up to take the helm of the Evans Corporation. Five years after the accident, life was settling into a predictable pattern. Her son and daughter were now 25. She should have been able to step back and relax with her son at the head of the corporation. But life wasn't going to let it be that easy. She should have known better.

A screech of tires on the front drive heralded the arrival of Liz. Kate tucked her memories away and hurried through the door to hug her glowing daughter. Elizabeth Katherine Evans Lansing was a younger version of her mother and was currently the possessor of a vastly expanded mid-section.

Both women gave evidence of an Irish heritage with their shining auburn hair and green eyes. While Kate was a slender five foot, eight inches, Liz possessed a frame that had more curves and was two inches shorter. Liz's sprinkling of freckles was more pronounced, and she had inherited her father's aristocratic nose.

Her normally cheerful disposition was markedly absent as she questioned her mother.

"Are you sure you don't want Jonathan to go with you?" she said.

"We've been over this a dozen times, darling," Kate replied patiently. "You're the one who needs your husband right now. You're going to have a baby in two months and I'll feel much better knowing he and Hugh are here to take care of you."

Liz scrunched up her nose and gave in with bad grace. "I suppose you're right, and I do know that my darling physics professor isn't going to be a great help to you on your search. When he gets distracted, he can forget where he is, but I'm just as worried about Michael as you are," she said. "After all, he is my twin."

"Yes, and there was a time when I would have called him the more dependable twin, but not now," Kate said as she slid into the passenger seat of her daughter's BMW.

"Since Jack's death and his own injuries in Viet Nam, his moods have become so unpredictable."

As Kate turned to take a last farewell of Hugh, Liz slid her growing belly behind the wheel. "Last chance; forget anything?" she queried.

Kate laughed and said, "You know perfectly well that there's no chance I'm going to remember anything I've missed at this point. That will only come later when I desperately need whatever I forgot. And, unfortunately, getting older is presenting more opportunities to do just that."

"We've got plenty of time, so I'm going to take the scenic route into New York," Liz said. "Since it's mid-day, we shouldn't have too much traffic."

"Do you want to stay at the apartment tonight?" Kate asked. "We could go to dinner tonight at the Jockey Club after I talk with Ted Sanders. Then you could go home tomorrow. I'm sure there are still enough clothes in your closets that we could kit you out."

"Thanks, but I think I'll go back this afternoon," Liz replied. "These days sleeping in my own bed seems more inviting, and my clothes at the apartment are mostly pre-baby so they are bound to be snug. Besides, Jonathan might actually notice if I wasn't there."

Kate was amused at Liz's references to her notoriously absent-minded, but brilliant young husband. She also knew that her daughter adored puttering around her new quarters.

The move from the big house where the Evans family had been so happy for 20 years had been a wrench. However, it was Kate who had insisted that it was the smart thing for all of them. Liz and Jonathan needed more room with the arrival of the baby.

After she spent several months redecorating the old coach house on their property, Kate had moved out of the imposing family home and left it to the kids to get on with the next generation. They still had a housekeeper, maid and gardener, so they weren't completely on their own. And Kate knew that whenever she was gone, Hugh was around, keeping an eye on things.

Her duties as chairman of the board kept her on the road quite often, so she didn't need all that space. The dozen companies that comprised the corporation ran well without her meddling, but she owed it to her employees and stockholders to put their interests foremost in her mind; second only to her family.

And that brought to her to the reason for this trip. In spite of all the plans and meetings that filled her time, Kate was desperately worried about her son, Michael. He had come home from Vietnam on a stretcher in 1973. A Viet Cong sniper with a Russian rifle had ended his military career.

The huge bullet had missed his heart but plowed through his shoulder, tearing tissue and nerves, as well as leaving a large cavity. It took months for the damage to heal and he came very close to losing his arm.

But it had healed and, with intensive rehab, he was tanned and healthy again. He'd finally started taking an interest in the business since he was the titular heir of that commercial behemoth. Liz had passed total control to him in favor of her art career.

There was something wrong beneath Michael's scars that he wouldn't discuss. He had been gone for a month and beyond a short call soon after he left, neither she nor Liz had heard anything from him. Kate had gotten tired of waiting and decided to go looking for him. Okay, he was a big boy. He and his sister had celebrated their 25th birthdays in April.

Regardless of his age, his mom knew something was festering and she wasn't going to put up with the silence anymore. Hence, the trip to Italy tomorrow night. He had planned to be there for a while and contact his father's dig foreman, Carlo Bernini. Where were they?

And then there was the second reason for her trip; the letter she'd found in Jack's desk. When she'd read its contents, she'd known she would have to go to Italy to find answers to the questions it raised. It presented an entirely new aspect of her husband's last trip; the one where he'd died in a tragic automobile accident.

"You've zoned off on me again," Liz said, startling Kate out of her reverie.

"Sorry," she said with a grin. "I know I check out from time to time when I'm thinking."

"I'm guessing it's Michael who's set you off this time," Liz stated. "You always were very closely attuned to his mental processes. That's truly why I'm worried now. As a twin, we're supposed to have some sort of unseen tether. But I know that you have a connection to Mike as well. So, if you've decided to go hunting, then I've decided to worry."

"I'm probably being an over-protective mother," Kate said lightly. "I don't want you to upset yourself over his lack of consideration for his family. He's a grown man with a real passion for his archeological work. It's easy to get involved and forget how much time has passed since he had his last hot meal, or bath, or phone call home. I'm sure he's fine. I just need to kick him a bit to remind him that he's going to have godfather duties in a very short time."

As if by mutual consent, the conversation turned to other topics. They ran through the list of things Liz would need to do while Kate was gone, especially concerning the new baby, and by the time they pulled up in front of the Evans' city apartment on Central Park West, both were in better moods.

Walter, the longtime doorman, opened Kate's door with a smile and said, "Good morning, Mrs. Evans. It's been a while since you and Miss Elizabeth visited us."

The Evans family had been in the same apartment off and on for more than 40 years. Jack's parents had been the first residents and divided their time equally between it and their home in Greenwich.

When Jack and Kate decided to make their home in New Haven, where Jack was a visiting lecturer, rather than Greenwich, they had still held on to the apartment for their frequent visits to New York. It was going to be useful as a rest stop for Kate before her Pan-Am flight the next night.

"Liz, come in and rest for a while before you drive back," Kate said. "Walter will see to parking the car. I need to dig out a few papers to take with me when I visit Ted Sanders. I can at least buy you lunch."

Kate led her into their top-floor apartment. The décor was the creation of Jack's mother, and Kate had never been sufficiently interested after she died to change anything. Antique rugs were scattered around the inlaid parquet floors. Silk drapes covered the windows to drown out any residual traffic noise.

The expansive living room was dotted with conversation areas complete with comfy sofas and small tables for drinks, lamps and books. A grand piano was situated in the center of the room. Her mother-in-law had been a gifted pianist and Liz was also very proficient.

Right now, Liz was flopped in a chair near the windows; her swollen ankles on a footstool and a picture-perfect view of the park outside.

"You know, when we were camping out in one of Dad's flea-infested digs with dirt and camel dung everywhere, this is the place I longed for most," she said poignantly.

Kate gave a shout of laughter. "You do realize that your father provided you with one of the most lavish lifestyles on the planet, don't you?" Kate inquired. "Yes, we found ourselves in some unusual settings, but we always had local staff as well as Hugh and Carlo to take care of you. Besides, you and your brother loved running wild."

"Yes, I guess we did," Liz admitted with a gleeful grin. "Mike got to help Dad the most, but I managed to learn exotic languages and customs that came in handy when the school year started. Some of those Arabic curse words really impressed the kids."

Kate vividly remembered the settings around the world where Jack; his foreman, Carlo Bernini; and Michael had worked together as an effective team from the time Michael was only 11. Because Michael had been seriously bitten by the archeological bug, their shared interest had been a close bond between father and son.

Those had been good times that had given purpose to all their lives. That was something Jack always searched for, an opportunity for the entitled family to make a difference. They not only brought employment to the diggers of six different sites, but also provided food for their families while the dig was active.

In addition, he was generous with the wives and children who got health care, dental work and new eyeglasses. He also managed to keep up with all of the families after the Evans family moved on. Several children were on educational scholarships from the Evans Foundation.

Carlo Bernini had left them when Jack finally decided to spend most of his time writing and teaching so the twins could have a more normal life. He also needed to be near New York. He was the heir to an estate that included more than a dozen companies with employees who depended on him to keep their paychecks coming.

His mother had filled that role while she was alive; allowing Jack to wander the earth with his family. But he'd taken the corporate helm when she died.

Jack had been alternately proud and devastated when Michael had volunteered for duty in Vietnam. Most of his peers had stampeded to get educational exemptions. Michael, who was probably the most serious scholar of the group, had felt the need to put in his time along with those who hadn't the money for a college deferment. He was his father's son.

Goodness knows Jack had fought valiantly to get into the war in the 1940s when everyone wanted him to stay home. But, in many ways, the war had made him the man he was. He had come home with a purpose – to save the world's art and architecture.

"I need to go over some things before I meet Ted," Kate said. "Do you want to eat lunch here or go out? I can call the deli down the street to deliver us something."

"If you don't mind, let's just eat in," Liz said. "I can put my swollen feet up for a while and you can do whatever you need to for Ted."

With that decided Kate went to her office and started pulling out foundation reports. The Kelly-Evans Foundation for the Arts was now one of the main recipients of the income from her investment portfolio. This had originally been Jack's baby, but as she had become more attuned to the business of finance and the needs of art institutions, she had joined as an equal partner.

When Jack died so suddenly, she had been glad she still had something so dear to his heart to occupy a good deal of her time. Among other things, the Foundation made grants to various artists; actively purchased art pieces from owners who wanted to divest their holdings; and donated most of the collection to various museums where they could be appreciated by public audiences. Everyone benefited.

Ted Sanders had been one of Jack's closest friends since their WWII Army days. Ted had volunteered to help with the MFAA program, and Jack had darted in and out of it, as needed. After the war, they'd both spent the last two years of their Army service rescuing art and architecture throughout Europe.

"I'll bet Uncle Ted will be glad to see you," Liz called from the living room.

"What do you mean?" Kate answered absently as she flipped another page of a report.

"Come on, Mom, even Michael noticed Uncle Ted's attitude toward you when he came home," Kate said.

Kate raised her head, now paying attention to her daughter.

"Liz, Ted and I have been friends for more than 30 years," Kate said. "If he seems glad to see me, it's just because we've been part of each other's lives forever. He's still grieving for Estelle. She's only been gone three years. I understand how he feels."

"I don't think you do," Liz said, leaning against the door of the office. "I don't remember Uncle Ted ever looking at Estelle the way he's looked at you. He's never seemed as sad without her as you are without Dad. I'll be very surprised if he doesn't ask you out to dinner when you see him. He's just been waiting to pounce."

"You make it sound like he's the cat and I'm the mouse," Kate said with a grin. "Somehow, I've never thought of myself that way. Don't you like Ted?"

Liz shrugged her shoulders. "I don't think I'd like to have him for a stepfather if you're thinking about filling that role," she said.

"Good heavens, Liz, I'm more than 50 years old," Kate exclaimed. "I have no intention to even date again, let alone marry anyone. Your father spoiled me. We were a marriage of partners. He was not only my husband and lover, but my best friend. When they told me the news of his death, I felt like an oak tree on a hill that had been split in half by lightning. Half of it was left to struggle on, but it would never be the same."

"Now the writer in you is coming out," Liz said quietly. "I know how hard this has been on you. I'd like to see you happy and loved again, Mom, I just don't think Ted is the right guy."

"Well, you certainly don't have to worry about that," Kate said with finality. "It would be like marrying my brother; no mystery and no surprises. And, I suspect he feels the same about me, so let's go eat."

She closed the portfolio on the desk and tucked it in a briefcase, then headed toward the dining room with Liz. The doorbell had announced the delivery of lunch.

Two hours later, her daughter was headed home and Kate was in a taxi on her way to the Foundation office on Wall Street. Jack had wanted his venture to have an address that would provide it with all the respect his projects deserved. That home was on the second floor of a marble building that had been around since the 1890s; no modern skyscrapers for him.

Tasteful blue-grey carpeting covered the floors. Mahogany reception desks and upholstered chairs were scattered around an area flooded with light from the floor-to-ceiling windows. Fresh arrangements of pink carnations, yellow ranunculus and cheerful white daisies sat on the tables. The crystal lamps provided a warm aura for reading.

Not that Kate had time to sit and read. As soon as she walked in, the receptionist picked up the phone to announce her arrival. Ted's secretary, Annie, appeared to usher her into his office.

He was on the phone when she sat down, so she had an opportunity to examine him without his being aware of her scrutiny. Ted was just a hair under six feet, with broad shoulders, dark hair, and a fair complexion. His eyes were brown and matched the color scheme set by his beige suit and brown silk tie from London's Savile Row.

He had come back to the United States about six months after Jack and immediately contacted him. His family in the

Midwest wanted Ted to come home to run the family business, but he was unwilling to go back to what he considered to be a quiet backwater. The war and his experiences with the Monuments Men had irrevocably changed him. He needed more challenges and excitement than Ohio had to offer.

Jack brought him into the Evans Corporation; then made him head of the Foundation when it was formed in 1952. His expertise was a mixture of business and art, which was just what Jack needed so Ted could run things when Jack wasn't around. When Jack died, Kate had left him in place. Two years later, Ted's wife had tragically drowned in their pool while Ted was in Paris.

They had both lost their partners, but Kate had never considered them more than friends. Was Liz right? Did Ted have other plans? Kate sincerely hoped he didn't, because she wouldn't want to hurt him or lose him as chief executive officer at the Foundation.

Sanders hung up the phone and turned to Kate. "Sorry, my dear, I had to finish that negotiation," he said. "The Met is deaccessioning its holdings of lesser-known Dutch artists to make room for more post-Impressionists and we've got a good shot at buying two or three. I've already got two small Midwestern museums targeted to receive them as donations."

"That's wonderful, Ted," Kate said. "That's the sort of redistribution of art that would have made Jack so proud."

"Yes, well, I always try to use his primary directive as my yardstick," Ted answered rather stiffly. "I also know there were other men who had more contacts within the art world that he could have chosen for this job."

"But Jack thought you'd be perfect as the executive director for the Foundation," Kate said. "You've got a head for business, but you also showed a passion for finding and returning lost art when you were with the Monuments Men. I remember how much time you spent with Baron Édouard de Rothschild's collection."

"Yes, that enormous collection took years to settle. I guess he was lucky to get out with his life; given what happened to other Jewish collectors," Ted said. "Most were sent to the extermination camps."

Then he gave a slight shake to his head and reached for a cigarette. He lit it, leaned back and said, "Well, I didn't mean to get us off on that topic, sorry. When does your plane leave and where are you staying in Rome?"

"I'm on Pan Am's late flight tomorrow night," Kate said. "I'm only spending one night in Rome, probably at the Hotel Cavalieri. I'm going to see a young woman who sent a letter to Jack about something that happened in San Sebastiano in 1946. She lives in Rome.

"At least I hope so. It seems like I've been running up blind alleys all week. I tried Michael again, but no luck. Then I phoned Carlo Bernini's home, but got no answer there. He could be anywhere in the world, but for some reason I was sure I'd find him in Rome."

"Maybe it's a sign you shouldn't go alone," Ted said. "If I didn't have the Met deal hanging fire right now, I'd give myself a vacation and go with you."

"No," Kate said. "I'd like to do this by myself. I'm sure I'll find Michael at some dig near Pompeii, completely unaware that I've been worried about him. I've got several other friends in Italy I can call on for assistance if I need it."

"OK," Ted said, raising his hands in surrender. "You're a big girl with lots of experience in some interesting places around the world. I'm sure you'll be fine but just remember I'm only a phone call away. Don't *you* lose contact with us. Call and let us know where you are, OK?"

"I will," Kate said. "I've gone over whatever events I have coming up before the next board meeting with Liz. She's my stand-in until I get back. You're handling the Foundation and the company presidents have all checked in with me this week, so all is well. This is a good time for me to be gone for a couple of weeks.

"Now, if you'll give me those contracts to sign, I'll get out of your hair. I have a little shopping to do, then home for an early night. A travel day is always tiring; more so as I've aged."

"My dear young lady," Ted began, "you don't look a day over 35 and I'll fight to the death anyone who says otherwise."

"Yeah, I'll bet," Kate said with a rueful laugh and picked up her pen.

An hour later, Ted Sanders was still sitting at his desk, pondering Kate's visit. He'd been in love with her since his first sight at her wedding to Jack. Old buddy Jack, who always seemed to have the best of everything: best wife, best education, best friends, best bank account, best luck

During the 10 years Ted had been married to Estelle, he'd just been going through the motions. He didn't think he'd been much more than a meal ticket to her, either. When she'd died in the drowning accident, Ted had waited patiently for Kate to turn to him.

It had been three years, but his patience was wearing thin. He had some personal business interests of his own, now, and he'd been thinking of leaving the Foundation to give them his attention. For now, his number one priority was Kate and her trip to Italy. When it was over, something had to change.

CHAPTER 3

Michael

Saigon, Vietnam
Apr 1975

Michael Evans squatted by the sagging window shutter on the second floor of the Phan house in Saigon. He peered carefully through a broken louver at the chaos below him. What had been despair had turned to panic and before long would be all-out mass hysteria.

The Viet Cong were closing the noose around the city. Soon there would be no escape for the hapless residents of the once proud Paris of the East.

The French would be hard pressed to recognize their former colony's capital. In their city, soft ocher-colored public buildings had graced streets filled with famous boutiques, decorated pubs and horse-drawn carriages. The Notre Dame Cathedral, the Central Post Office and the Grand and Majestic hotels had given the city a European flair like no other place in Asia.

The city had suffered through WWII during the Japanese occupation and the corrupt governance by the

French Vichy puppets, but it had survived. It might have been a bit wild in the 1950s when Graham Greene lived there while writing *The Quiet American*, but it was a beautiful and cosmopolitan hodgepodge of Asian and Western cultures.

When the Americans descended on it in 1965, the word culture no longer applied in any form. The city became a morass of cheap bars, drugs and sexual excess, completely unaware of any impending doom.

Payday had arrived, Michael thought – in spades. Now everyone was looking for a place to hide. Where was Danh? He should have been back hours ago. Michael risked another quick glimpse at the street below. He knew that among the raging crowds moving aimlessly through the city, there would be a few who could recognize him.

He might have left 18 months ago, but he'd met a lot of people during those last weeks in Saigon when he acted as a military attaché at the American embassy. Some of them would know he wasn't supposed to be here and wonder how he'd gotten in. More importantly, they'd wonder how he was getting out; that's why he'd moored the boat so far away.

He certainly shouldn't be here as a private citizen. There was no government safety net if Viet Cong insurgents recognized him. Even his family didn't know he was here. He'd sworn his secretary to secrecy, but if things went sideways on this venture, he was on his own. The last thing he wanted to do was attract attention.

Below, he heard the cautious scrape of a door opening and waited; then he saw Danh's face appear at the top of the stairs.

"Where have you been, Danny?" he asked impatiently.

"Man, it's almost impossible to get anything done out there," Danh replied in colloquial English.

Michael could remember when Danh, a snotty-nosed brat with constantly stained clothes, had proudly followed the Army Rangers under Michael's command around the city, along with a gang of three other boys. Now he was nearly 15 and had to bear the burden of rounding up whatever family members he could to make one last escape attempt. Everyone was running out of time.

"Did you see any sign of people watching this house?" Michael inquired.

"Everything is such a mess out there I probably wouldn't recognize anyone unless he held up a sign," Danh admitted. "I don't think anyone is interested in us. Right now, it's every man for himself."

Michael hoped Danh was right. People were loading onto every junk, sampan and row boat they could find to get out of the country. He'd left the freighter, the *S.S. Kelly Dear,* anchored twelve miles off the coast in territorial waters. He and a small crew had sailed up the Mekong on a junk that was moored on the river a mile from the city. Sooner or later, it was sure to attract unwanted attention. Questions were going to be asked and word of its presence would spread.

When Michael left Saigon on a stretcher, he hadn't planned to return. But he'd promised young Danh that he'd make arrangements for him and his family to receive visas to leave Vietnam as soon as he got home.

The Phan family had been kind to him. Danh's father, Lanh Minh, had been an interpreter at the American Embassy. His mother, a lovely lady named Mai An, had made bountiful meals whenever Michael came for dinner. Along with Danh's younger sister, Jade, they had opened their home to him on countless occasions. There was no way he was leaving any of them behind for whatever the Viet Cong had in store for the conquered people of Saigon.

Back in the states, he'd discovered that a large evacuation wasn't going to be as easy as he'd thought. Even with the backing of the Evans' money and highly placed friends in Washington, picking more than dozen people out of Saigon and putting them on the priority list wasn't going to happen quickly.

He thought he would have more time, of course. When he left, the Viet Cong were making some headway south, but at no great speed. Then American troops began to be pulled out in greater numbers and the young Vietnamese army left in their place wasn't able to hold the line.

Michael decided he'd have to do something quickly and had arranged to commandeer one of the Evans Oil Company's supply freighters in the Philippines to make the trip across the South China Sea. He'd had another reason, too, for coming back, though not as pressing. Yes, he wanted

Danh and the Phan family out of this hell, but he also wanted to ask a certain Dutchman a few questions. He'd had that chance last night, but it had ended in disappointment.

"What about your Granny? Is she coming here?" Michael asked.

"No, I've made arrangements for the aunties and uncles to take her to the fishing village where the junk is anchored. My father's sister has a house there and will keep them hidden until we can get them aboard. I told them we'd be there by 17:00 hours and slip aboard the ship after dark. Granny isn't happy about abandoning Saigon, but since Dad is now head of the family, she had to listen to him," Danh answered.

Michael was wryly amused that the boy still told time in military form although the soldiers had been out of his life for months. Danh had hero-worshiped the men because of their rough kindness in giving him candy bars and the occasional nickel or dime. It was a small amount to the Americans, but hugely important to Danh.

In repayment, he'd given them scraps of information he picked up on the streets. One such tip had led to the evacuation of a Marine barrack before a bomb planted by an infiltrator had exploded. Since Michael's platoon had been quartered there, Danh was always going to be on Michael's Christmas card list.

"Well, Danny boy, we should be going, too," Michael said at last. He'd been thinking about the best way to blend in with the crowds, but that was going to be hard. His appearance was going to stand out now more than at any time since the American Embassy had closed its gates.

Danh, though, had given a great deal of thought to his disguise. Michael stood more than six feet tall in his socks. He had a flaming head of hair and Irish features that also pegged him as an outsider, especially the bright blue eyes he'd inherited from his father, Jack.

Danh had brought a wide-brimmed straw hat with graying hair glued inside the brim, which covered Michael's startling red mane. Old pants and a long-sleeved shirt covered his fair-skinned arms and legs.

He'd have to leave his boots behind, but the old pair of broken leather shoes with flapping soles would protect his feet somewhat and still cover his tell-tale skin color. He didn't even want to think about who had worn them last or where the hair on the hat came from. The disguise was completed by a pair of bent-rimmed glasses that hung mostly from one ear.

"You won't be able to move too fast," Danh said, "and the shoes will make you hunch forward to keep them on. That will help make you shorter." He was obviously proud of his enterprise and Michael smiled his thanks.

"Let's go, Danny. You stay about five feet in front of me. Act like you're alone. If anyone catches me out in the open, let me worry about them and you go on to your family. When you get to the junk, tell Captain Farrell that Michael says, 'All's well that ends well.' That's the code that will tell him you're with me. He'll take it from there," Michael instructed as Danh nodded solemnly.

As they started down the stairs, Michael wished that they could have waited until dark, but it would take them at least an hour to walk to the fishing village. The size of the crowds and the unexpected violence that was breaking out as people became desperate would also impact their progress.

As he walked along, his thoughts turned to recent events. In the months after he returned home, wounded and depressed, his mother and sister had smothered him with love and attention, but his mood had been dark. He'd been troubled by memories of his time in combat.

Once he'd recovered from his wound and completed rehab, he felt a desperate need to be free to wander; to find something useful to do. He'd spent too long as his father's chief aide on the many archeological sites they'd explored to be content sitting by the pool.

He decided to contact his father's site foreman, Carlo Bernini, in Italy about doing some excavating in Greece. There were still one or two islands with sites that hadn't been completely explored and he thought this would distract him. He deeply felt the loss of his father while he'd been in Viet Nam. Along with Uncle Carlo, they'd made a great team.

When he got Carlo on the phone, he was surprised to hear that Carlo wanted him to come to Rome, as quickly as he could. He didn't want to discuss it over the phone, but he'd discovered some disturbing information concerning Jack Evans last visit, the one that had cost him his life.

Michael's private plane had no more than touched the ground when Carlo had him out of the airport and hustled into a trattoria a few streets from the Trevi Fountain. There, Carlo introduced him to the reason for the hurried trip; a man named Dominic. He didn't give his last name. Carlo urged Michael to sit and listen.

"My grandfather was one of Mussolini's Blackshirts," Dominic began without preamble. "He believed in Il Duce to the end and wanted to help, even after the Americans and British had landed in Italy and were heading for Rome. He was very angry that the Allies had bombed Naples and destroyed so many of the beautiful buildings and monuments. My mother told me all this," he said, by way of explanation.

Michael poured him a little more of the rough red wine to encourage him to continue.

"My grandfather was asked by his Blackshirt friends to take on a secret mission. They wanted him to guide some Germans to a town outside of Naples called San Sebastiano al Vesuvio. Anything that would help the Germans would, he believed, hurt the Americans, so he said yes. I don't think he knew what they were going to do – at least he didn't tell my grandmother when he left to meet them. She never saw him again," Dominic said in a tightly controlled voice.

"It all happened a long time ago, but recently, while I was working on repairing the town hall in San Sebastiano, an old man who was part of my grandfather's Blackshirt unit came up to me and told me about that last trip. He had remained silent for all these years through fear; he always thought those involved were Americans.

"But a recent newspaper story about a find in the church crypt indicated that the bodies had been German. He thought I should know now. The Germans were transporting something in a truck and my grandfather drove the truck."

Mildly interesting, Michael thought; but he was still puzzled at Carlo's insistence that he hear all this.

"All this happened during the time Vesuvius was exploding, you know," Dominic said. "Almost all the village was empty when they came, but this man had stayed till the end to guard the family's house across from the church. He had stayed much longer than he should have, but he saw my grandfather drive the truck to the church. Then soldiers were carrying things inside. Pretty soon two of them came out and my grandfather drove them away.

"The man thinks they might have killed the others; because later he heard about workers finding bodies in the church. I believe they killed my grandfather to keep secret what they did," he concluded abruptly.

Now it was Carlo's turn to surprise him.

"Michael, Dominic just learned all this recently. He lives in Naples, but has a cousin in Rome. He told the cousin what he'd learned, and the cousin told my sister. She mentioned it to me last week because she knew of my interest in that town," Carlo said.

Knowing full well how the Italian neighborhood telegraph system worked, Michael gave Carlo the hurry-up sign with his hand.

"When your father was in Italy after the war, he went to San Sebastiano al Vesuvio at the request of General Eisenhower's staff to see if he could help with that church. He told me so when he came through Rome that last time.

"He was going back because of a letter he'd received. There seemed to be some mystery about the death of the old priest he'd met, and the housekeeper. The letter was from the housekeeper's niece. He was on his way there when he had his car accident," Carlo said.

He paused, then said, "I've never understood that accident. It was a clear night and your father had driven the road before. It's narrow, but flat, no hills or dangerous curves. Because of your family's influence, the Italian authorities checked the car for any mechanical problems, but found nothing wrong. There was no reason for the car to go off the road and crash, unless someone or something deliberately made him swerve."

Michael sat quietly stunned for a few seconds, trying to take it all in. "You mean you think someone caused the accident; killed him on purpose?" he asked incredulously. Carlo nodded quickly.

"Not only that," Carlo continued. "But I've checked. The niece is dead, too. Has been for five years; just before Jack's accident."

The jostling Saigon crowds briefly brought him back to the present. He'd been anxious to continue the discussion with Carlo and Dominic but he received a message from his secretary that Danh was trying to get in touch with him. That could only mean that they were running out of time.

He'd hurriedly organized the rescue trip, all the while remembering the other thing he wanted to check on while he was here. The painting.

In 1973, he'd been standing in a hallway at the Ecole de Beaux-Arts de l'Indochine, a shining remnant of its years as a French colony. On the wall of the famous art school was a painting of such luminous beauty that he had been unable to turn away from it.

Caught in the radiant sunshine was the figure of a man in a straw hat walking on a road. He held a painter's easel under one arm. The blue-green sky, the trees, the golden wheat field and the general aura of warmth radiated off the small canvas. His shadow wandered behind him and danced across the roadway. Clearly this was something from the Impressionist school that had preceded the war and just as clearly, it had been painted by a master.

Michael was awestruck. He had been waiting with an invitation from his general to the school's director, Francois Benet, to join them that night at a reception for some Washington dignitary. The painting had attracted him from 20 feet away.

"Stunning, isn't it?" Benet inquired.

"Yes. Who painted it?" Michael asked.

"One of our patrons went to Paris for art school before WWII and acquired it there. I'm not sure who did it," Benet said.

"When did it come here?" Michael asked.

"I don't know. It was here when I came 15 years ago," Benet said as he turned to walk away.

He stopped short; then turned back to Michael. "You might inquire of Pieter Van Hooten. He's our resident European art expert," Benet said. "He's a Dutch planter who lives about an hour downriver. I imagine he might even have known the student who brought it back."

When one of life's coincidences brought him in contact with Van Hooten later that night at the Embassy party, he had taken the Dutchman aside to ask about the painting.

"It's a fine copy, isn't it? The original was by a Dutch painter," Van Hooten said. "I believe the copy was made by young Nguyen Binh, an extremely talented Vietnamese artist. I knew him slightly in Paris before the war.

"It was his raptures over the beauty of Viet Nam that helped me decide to move here. Coming here was a fortuitous move on my part. I found fertile land, dependable workers and great contentment."

The Dutchman was very much on his mind as he shuffled slowly along in his flapping shoes. He'd discovered the painting was no longer on display at the Ecole, and he had no luck trying to find anyone from the faculty. Then he'd contacted Van Hooten requesting a meeting. Somewhat to his surprise, Van Hooten had agreed to meet him for a few minutes last night at a rundown local hotel.

Pieter Van Hooten, formerly known as German SS Lt. Karl Hesse, was sitting in the shabby room when a knock on the door heralded Michael's arrival. Hesse called for him to enter and then waited for Michael to open the conversation.

"I want to talk about the painting at the Ecole," he said brusquely.

Hesse produced a smile that never reached his eyes.

"Yes, and good evening to you, too, Mr. Evans," he said.

"I'm not interested in fencing with you tonight," Michael continued. "I've got too many things going on, but I want to know what's happened to it."

Hesse was silent for a long minute, then apparently made up his mind. He straightened in his chair and gestured to the one across from his. "Take a seat, young man, because this is going to take a while. Would you care for some cognac?" he asked.

Michael just shook his head and settled for a rattan armchair. Hesse sat silent for some moments, then he began.

"It is singularly amazing that our paths have crossed this way," he said. "I've never been a great believer in Kismet, but this is the Far East so where else would you find it. You've taken me back 30 years, to a time when I was a 27-year-old lieutenant in the Nazi SS.

"As an art student before the war, I had traveled a good deal. I spoke English and French, and I knew a good deal about the contents of some of Europe's most famous art collections. All in all, it made me an ideal candidate for a specialized program in Paris. There I coordinated the gathering and shipping of seized materials from those same collections to Germany and the Führer's friends," he said.

"I was much more of a dilettante than a dedicated Nazi, although one does learn to be harsh by necessity when surrounded by those exercising power through force," he continued.

"My unit oversaw the confiscation at all the fabulous homes in Paris and the surrounding countryside. My special favorites were the Rothschild homes. They were filled with such unbelievably beautiful things that I was in my own special heaven cataloging and packing them for shipment," he said, shaking his head at the memories.

He shifted slightly in his chair, obviously hitting a thought that was not quite as pleasant.

"We were very efficient. We were nearing completion of our project, carefully packing things and putting them in box cars for transport to Germany. Suddenly I received orders to pull specific items from the inventory and prepare them for shipping in waterproof, airtight containers."

"What kind of things?" Michael asked.

"Paintings, beautiful paintings that could be rolled and put in metal tubes." Hesse said. "That meant leaving their historic and valuable frames behind. The total package had to be something that could fit easily through a submarine hatch. In the end, we needed 20 of these cannisters for all the paintings if they weren't to be destroyed by rolling. Too tight and they would have been forever creased."

Hesse took a fortifying swallow of cognac and continued. "I was personally to escort these to a submarine off the French coast and stay with them until they were unloaded onto a fishing smack in Italian waters. Then I was to travel with them to the town of Portici. This was spring of 1944 and the Allied troops were all over southern Italy.

"Since I was going into enemy-held territory, I would be leaving my uniform and my protection as a German officer behind. If caught, I would be shot as a spy. If I failed to obey orders, I would be shot as a traitor. Not that it was so crudely put, but it was implied," he said with irony.

"In the end, I not only had to escort them to the fishing boat, but also to go ashore and meet a unit of German soldiers. We were going to escort the paintings to a small church near Vesuvius," he added.

Michael's face tightened as he suddenly realized where this story was leading. It was part of the story Carlo's friend Dominic had told. Talk about coincidence.

"I rendezvoused with the unit whose commander was a rather forbidding SS officer from Hitler's staff. I didn't find that out until later, and I'm glad. If I'd known then who he was, I'd probably have jumped overboard before we docked," Hesse admitted with a grimace.

"In any case, I was there. There was the Colonel, a tough sergeant, and four of the worst-looking privates I had ever seen. They were strong, though, and we got my cannisters unloaded and stored in the fishing shed. There was also another item, more of a steel box, but Colonel Lang took care of it all the time. They had actually stolen a US Army truck, and everyone was to wear US Army uniforms.

"I spoke English, as did the Colonel. Funnily enough, so did two of the privates and the sergeant. They'd grown up in the US after immigrating there in the Twenties. They moved back to Germany to fight for the Fatherland. Can you imagine? But if we'd been stopped, we could have had a great conversation with the GIs," he said with a slight laugh.

"Then things began to go wrong, as far as I was concerned," he recalled. "Mt. Vesuvius has these eruptions every so often, and it was in the midst of one of these as we drove straight toward it. The roads got worse and worse. The local driver knew where he was going, and thank God for that. There was no other traffic. Nobody else was stupid enough to be outside. Rocks were being hurled in the air along with lava and that noxious, choking sulfur that gagged everyone.

"We were going to a little town at the base of the mountain, San Sebastiano al Vesuvio. When we finally arrived at an old church, we were quick to open it up, get everything inside, and move the main altar. There was a crypt under it that was going to be the resting place of the treasures we were carrying. When everything was inside, the Colonel signaled the sergeant, and he started killing the men in the crypt. I wasn't prepared," he paused.

"I could not believe we were killing our own men. But there was more to come. As soon as the privates were taken care of, the Colonel turned his gun on the sergeant. I was sure I was going to be next, but he just yelled for me to help him relocate the crypt door and the altar," Hesse concluded.

"It appears you got out of there okay," Michael finally noted. "You also appear to have evaded any punishment for your part in the episode."

Hesse said, "Yes. I have little memory of getting back to the coast, probably because I thought the Colonel would kill me and dump me in the ocean. Finally, though, I got back to Paris to finish my job there and decided I was done with the Führer.

"As I once told you, I came in contact with a young French-Vietnamese man who'd encouraged me to visit Viet Nam. When I was ready to relocate in the closing weeks of the war, the chief attraction was its obscurity. I thought it might be the last place on earth anyone would look for a Nazi. And, it was."

"Your comment about Kismet seems to be prescient," Michael said. "Just before I came here, I received word that a witness to your visit to San Sebastiano saw everything you've described. He'd remained silent because he believed you really were Americans and he'd get into trouble because he'd failed to evacuate the village when ordered. He also knew your driver. Since the driver never returned home, I presume either you or this Colonel killed him, too," Michael said.

"Yes, the Colonel took care of the driver in the same way I thought he'd kill me – a bullet in the head and a quick dump in the ocean," Hesse said.

"What was the Colonel's name?" Michael asked.

"It was Werner Lang. He was a special aide to Hitler. I have heard rumors that he survived the war and is now prospering as a merchant of war; selling arms to both sides. He was one of the most cold-blooded bastards I've ever met, and I knew a lot of SS and Gestapo brutes. He shot the sergeant right in front of me, said it was 'orders' but he enjoyed it," Hesse said.

Michael filed this name away and continued.

"I have a special interest in this because my father, Jack Evans, died in an auto accident near San Sebastiano five years ago. He was on his way to meet a woman who'd written him a letter. She claimed that the priest and his housekeeper had both been murdered, presumably by the men who'd opened the crypt. You and Lang seem to be the only others still living who know exactly what was left there. Do you know what happened to the cargo?" he asked.

"No, I don't, but from a few of the names I saw on the packing list, it was the cream of the crop from the seized Italian paintings. Caravaggio, Raphael, Botticelli, Michelangelo – all things that would be worth many, many millions today, even on the black market.

"If they're not in the tomb anymore, since Mussolini didn't live long enough to retrieve them, Lang must have taken them. I'll tell you this; Lang's not the type to share. He'll kill anyone who gets in his way, or might get in his way," Hesse said, his clenched fist hitting the chair arm for emphasis.

Michael silently mulled what Hesse had said.

Hesse continued, "There was something else that Mussolini badly wanted in that steel box. I don't know what it was, it wasn't on the manifest. I remember seeing it open just once. Lang was checking the contents while the troops were loading the crypt. Besides a treasure trove of small jeweled items, there was an envelope – just letter-sized; not thick. I thought it was a strange item to keep company with all the other treasures we were transporting."

He leaned back in his chair. "I have no actual proof that he's still alive. My coterie of informants has diminished with the years. However, as late as February, I heard that the Colonel was in Yugoslavia. Like me, he was young for his position in the SS. He would only be in his mid-sixties now. If he has been keeping watch over the crypt or wherever its contents ended up, I would not be surprised. The cargo was very valuable and easily portable. If your father got in his way, Lang would not have hesitated to eliminate him, no matter how prominent he was.

"If you plan to investigate what happened to your father, be aware that you will be in danger. The Colonel will stop at nothing to further his plans, whatever they are. Your father may have been in the wrong place at the wrong time. The Colonel may simply have removed him. He could do it again – probably will," he concluded.

"All right, I will deal with all this when I return to Rome. I'll launch a full-scale investigation of Lang and his activities. But what about the painting at the Ecole? Was it a Van Gogh?" Michael asked.

"Ah yes, that painting. I knew that I'd made a mistake exhibiting it the minute you mentioned seeing it. But it was so lovely. It was one of three I acquired before I left Paris. German soldiers were burning the Impressionists, so I knew no one would miss them. Money from the Switzerland sale of the first two paid for my passage here, purchased the land and bought me a number of informants in the right places. The last one, I donated to the Ecole. No one knew how valuable it was. I brought it home after you left," he said.

"But where is the Ecole's painting now? Is it safe?" Michael asked.

"No. I'm sorry. I didn't know you would be coming back to rescue it, and I didn't want the Viet Cong to get it. I did what I was supposed to do 30 years ago. I burned it out at my plantation. And, yes, it was a Van Gogh called *Painter on the Road to Tarascan*," he said sadly.

Michael winced as Hesse baldly described the fate of that incredible painting.

In the silence, Hesse said, "I'm leaving Asia, but I haven't decided yet on another destination. I, too, have a ship waiting, but I won't be taking much baggage with me. There was no room for the painting. I've spent a small fortune bribing one of the ship's officers to include me in their last voyage. I seem to be an expert at bribing people. Let's hope this one is more successful than my last effort.

"I go tomorrow. If you want to get out of here alive, you'd better be gone soon, too. Wouldn't the Viet Cong just love to get their hands on you. How many millions do you think your family would have to pay to rescue you – the very wealthy Mr. Evans, head of the Evans Corporation?"

Both men stood. Neither extended a hand. Hesse gave a nod of his head and opened the door.

"Obviously, I'm not going to be around here any longer than I can help," Michael said. "I plan to get to my boat first thing tomorrow and start down the Mekong tomorrow night. As soon as I can get within helicopter range of a major airport, I'll leave the ship and head for Italy. I'm going to be looking for answers now. I abhor the things you did, but I am grateful that you told me why my father might have been murdered."

Jerked out of his memories of the previous night by the increased clamor, Michael knew he was within a block of the American embassy. A helicopter circled before landing on the embassy rooftop, quickly filled and lifted off.

Marines still held off the crowds with their guns, but a few Westerners were allowed to climb the fencing to get inside the compound. As each one disappeared over the wall, the roar grew. Would the helicopters be able to take everyone inside the compound?

At some point, they would have to stop. A time limit had been agreed to by the American government and the Viet Cong. Now the enemy was literally just outside the city. With virtually no opposition, they were hurrying toward a goal they'd long coveted.

Another half-hour brought them to the fishing village of Phuong Duc. Danh stopped at his aunt's home and quickly gathered up the family. These emigres carried a pitifully few belongings to begin a new life, but they were grateful to go.

As they herded the small flock another quarter of a mile to the dock, Michael constantly checked over his shoulder. The crew of the ship was alert and hurried to lower a gangplank. Michael stood watch as Danh helped old Granny and the aunts and uncles as they slowly crossed to the boat.

The minute Danh and his parents stepped on deck, Michael cast off the mooring line and gave the signal. The heavily-laden blue junk sailed five minutes later, finding a way through the blockades along the river to clear water and a quick run to Manilla on the big freighter. Michael needed to see Uncle Carlo again.

CHAPTER 4

Dair

Scottish Highlands
8 May, 1975

Alisdair Munro, known to his friends and enemies alike as Dair, stood under the old pine tree five yards from his Uncle Angus' front door. Inside the house, the old man lay fighting his last battle.

Dair stood perfectly still, as did everything around him; no wind tonight; no rain in the air. It was as if everyone and everything in the glen was holding its breath. He did, however, wish he had a cigarette. Nearly 30 years after giving them up, he still missed one occasionally. His uncle had broken him of that habit very soon after he came to live with him. There was too much chance of being observed if the glowing tip of a cigarette gave you away in the dark.

There was no end to the things Angus had hammered into and out of him during those first years. The scrappy kid from County Tipperary had come to Scotland to live with his uncle when Dair's father died in a racing accident – horses, not cars. His mother, Angus' sister-in-law, was just about

able to manage the family stud farm and his three sisters –
but not him. Something had to give, and she had sent a
protesting 12-year-old to the rough and ready care of a living
legend.

Angus Munro owned almost every medal and award that
Britain, France, Belgium and the Netherlands could bestow
on one man. Of course, he never wore them. He didn't even
like to wear a uniform. Very soon, those medals, the house,
and the care of this branch of the Clan Munro would become
Dair's responsibility. He was the laird's heir. The 13th in a
long line of lairds. He was also more than a little concerned
about that fact.

As he neared 52, he was used to being in charge of just
one life; that of Alisdair Munro. Angus had always managed
all the peripheral parts of Dair's life, leaving him free to
pursue the things that interested him; such as trying to keep
the bad guys from getting the upper hand.

His service with Interpol had changed the lives of
thousands of people who were impacted by the trafficking of
drugs, slaves and military arms. That was all about to
change. Upstairs, the man who'd helped him make sense of
life on countless occasions lay dying.

He saw the outer door begin to swing open; then Quinn
O'Malley stepped outside.

"Dair," Quinn murmured quietly. Dair stepped into the
light cast by the open door. This was the summons he'd been
dreading.

"The doctor is getting ready to leave. He wants to talk to you," Quinn reported.

Dair slipped inside and waited for Doctor Ferguson, who'd patched him up since he was a kid, to come down the stairs.

"He's drifting in and out, but he wants to see you. I'm glad you managed to get here when you did. I don't think it will be much longer," the doctor said, not bothering to sugar-coat the news. He was dealing with men who didn't go in much for sugar.

"What happened?" Munro asked. "This seems to have come on awfully fast."

"It wasn't fast," Ferguson replied tartly. "He's been sick for almost a year. He just kept lying to himself – and to you – because he's always subscribed to the theory that he was immortal. God knows that old Celt has come as close to immortal as anybody I've ever known."

Munro smiled wryly, agreeing with the doctor. Angus had always been larger than life and he'd changed the future for more lives than any of them could count.

He turned slowly, conscious of the fact that he hadn't slept in two days, and climbed the stairs. Angus' door was open. The light from the bedside lamp spilled over the man on the bed, highlighting the sharp planes of his still-rugged face. It also gave evidence of the man's extreme height. However, there was a new suggestion of frailty about him that Dair had never seen before. The doctor was right, this hadn't happened in just the three weeks since he'd last talked with Angus by phone.

As he took the chair next to the bed, Angus cracked open an eye and gave a grimace that passed for a smile.

"So, they dragged you home, did they, laddie?" he said with some difficulty. "I told them to leave you be. I know this project needs your complete attention."

"I was due for some leave, anyway." Dair responded casually. "You know I always like to spend time here when I get the chance.

Angus responded gruffly, "Don't try to bullshit me, Alisdair; I've always known when you were lying. And the last thing I want is you wasting time sitting some kind of death vigil when there are much more important things you should be doing." As he spit out each of the words, his Scottish brogue became more pronounced. That was never a good sign.

"I don't plan to sit around here very long, so relax," Dair countered. "I truly did need some rest before I tackle the next part of this mess. I've left some good men investigating things in France and Italy. My sources tell me things are heating up. I'll need to get back in about three days because one of the main players is coming to Italy.

"Her son seems to have dropped out of sight and Mama Bear isn't happy. I need to be back on the scene when she gets there because I think her presence will cause some movement. It may be time to let her in on what's been going on with her Foundation."

Angus was silent for a few moments, then opened his eyes again.

"This has gone on too long. It's 1975 for God's sake and this all began in 1945! This has cost too many innocent lives. I don't want yours to be one of them," he said. With that outburst, he seemed to exhaust his anger and again drifted off.

Dair sat beside the bed, remembering the first time he'd seen Angus – the Munro, Laird of Glenronan. At 12, he'd been a cocky Mick, even if both his parents were Scots, born in Glenronan. His parents had owned a small stud farm there, where he'd been born in 1923. He was the youngest, with three older sisters.

After the family moved to Ireland when he was a toddler, he'd been his father's shadow, always with him as he worked with the horses and foals on their new farm. His father's death in a riding accident when he was 10 had rocked him badly. His mother had been distracted, trying to keep the stud operating and raising four devastated children. He'd gone looking for something different in his life and had run right into the local IRA Provos.

He found them exciting and masculine at a time when the females in his life were smothering him. As a lookout and messenger boy, he'd had a few small scrapes until the local constable in Cashel had pulled him up short and taken him home. When the extent of his involvement was revealed to his mother, she was unnervingly silent.

He knew she was disappointed, aghast and angry, all at the same time. His sisters were instructed to keep him with them at all times, and his sisters were horrendous busybodies. If he was two minutes late meeting them to walk home after school, the entire town would know about it.

That short rein began to wear on all of them and it wasn't long before his mother made a decision that must have been as painful for her as it was for him. He was leaving. Period. No discussion. He was going to Scotland! She'd just as well have said Siberia.

He was going to live with his uncle, his father's older brother, Angus Munro. Uncle Angus was a legend he'd heard about as long as he could remember. Angus would have complete discretion over his life from then on and God help him if he didn't shape up.

He recalled his first sight of Angus as the Dublin ferry docked in Liverpool. He'd made the trip down from the Highlands to pick Dair up. As they appraised each other on the pier, neither was sure they liked what they saw. Dair was growing fast and was in the midst of the gawky phase that all pre-pubescent males seemed to go through – definitely not a promising sight. He was tired, sad and desperately missed his family, even though he'd die before admitting that.

Angus towered over him at 6 feet 6 inches. He was built like a brick wall, with muscles rippling beneath his fisherman's sweater. He had black hair, black eyes and a black scowl.

They both knew he could pick Dair up by the scruff of his neck and dump him back in the Irish Sea if he'd wanted. For some reason, he didn't. He signaled Dair to pick up his bags and follow him. He didn't offer to help carry them.

That began a long period of Dair trying to measure up to Angus' standards and usually falling short. In 1940, they'd had a knock-down-drag-out fight over Dair joining the British Army. He lost.

He'd found out that Angus had been only 17 when he sneaked off to join the British forces in France during World War I. By the time the war was over, he'd distinguished himself enough to have the name 'hero' attached to his name. Angus had other plans for Dair.

Following WWI, the British military had wanted to keep Angus. However, he was a landowner in Scotland and was conscious of what he owed his people. Back in the Highlands, he set up a training camp that attracted men who wanted to learn more about martial arts, commando strategy, and other talents that weren't being provided in a country that had already fought the 'war to end all wars.'

But as the British military was downsizing its army and navy, Adolf Hitler started making noise in Europe. By the mid-1930s, Angus Munro's talents became more valuable. He was invited to offer advice to the British military on the less gentlemanly aspects of warfare.

By 1940, he was running a full-scale military encampment on his estate for a select group of trainees the War Department sent him. Inevitably, Dair learned these skills along with the other trainees. He thought he'd have to argue with Angus to let him train, but his uncle had surprisingly agreed, as long as he kept up with his academic studies. Angus had definite opinions about wasting a good brain.

In fact, he had opinions about everything. Dair learned that it was wise to respect them. His uncle was never brutal with him, but he was firm and fair. Dair blossomed under his tutelage.

Before long, Angus was asked to take on the training of US Army ranger units. These were a new addition to the American armed forces. The units were made up of older, tougher volunteers who were looking for a different kind of war. This wasn't the freckle-faced boy-next-door, hoping to get home soon type. It was more likely the roughneck-next-door who was looking for a fight variety.

Angus drove them unmercifully, teaching them to track and kill silently. Soon, he was asked to teach them to climb tall mountains. In this entire endeavor, Dair had been by his side. The push to have them ready by D-Day resulted in crack battalions, not seen in any traditional war before. Units with the names Darby's Rangers and Rudder's Rangers would become known through the international headlines.

Angus not only assisted in getting rangers ready to climb Pointe du Hoc on D-Day, June 6, 1944, but he also took to the beaches of Normandy on that day to offer whatever assistance he could.

Dair's only disappointment was that the war ended before he could see action. Angus had no intention of letting him sneak off at age 17, as he had done. With the end of the war, Dair found himself installed at St. Andrew's University to continue his education. When he finished there, he traveled the world with his uncle, who had become a military advisor to various armies.

He took Dair with him to assist since he'd become expert at hand-to-hand combat; could shoot any type of firearm; had command of a number of languages; and was talented with a knife. He was the quintessential killing machine, but he had never used any of his gifts for anything but instructing others.

When the Korean War came along, he joined the NATO forces with a group of British commandos and advanced to the rank of captain. All in all, it hadn't been too bad, although he didn't like the rules and the Brits weren't overly fond of a captain who was a Scot with an Irish accent. He didn't have an easy time, but his men grew to respect him. The respect was earned due to the remarkably few casualties in his command.

That's where he'd met Quinn O'Malley, a daring and irreverent Irishman. They'd bonded over a bottle of Jamieson whiskey. Quinn had become a permanent fixture in the Munro clan.

After Korea, it had taken a while to sort out his life. He'd used all that hard-earned training, but it hadn't been a satisfying experience. He finally realized he didn't have the killer instinct.

In fact, he wanted to experience the academic world again. With a small shove from Angus, he went to Cambridge to study art history – about as far from professional mercenary as he could get.

His acquaintance with the French and Italian languages had fostered a curiosity about their cultures. This led to their storied histories in the arts – painting, sculpture, music, literature. He devoured it all.

In doing so, he also found out in great detail what had happened to many of those art treasures at the hands of the Nazis. Some of the men and women who had worked to find and restore those European treasures had come from Cambridge. He admired the work they and their American counterparts had done.

When a great personal tragedy destroyed the measured tranquility of his Cambridge life, he had been ripe for a drastic change. That's when friends of friends had started to feel out his willingness to take on a new challenge. Representatives from Interpol approached him with their project.

As they explained how the past was still affecting the present and tried to enlist his aid, he found a renewed interest in living. He wasn't going to join Interpol – too many rules – but he was willing to give them his services as a contract advisor and consultant.

They weren't happy, but they settled for what they could get. The deal also included one Quinn O'Malley.

They'd had a very successful partnership; solving dozens of cases in multiple countries. They closed down several large cartels and sent nine kingpins to prison for the rest of their lives. He wasn't blind to the fact that others would replace them, but he made a difference where he could and settled for that. With the death of Angus, this latest case would be their last.

Dair came to with a jolt, realizing he'd been dozing in the chair. There had been a change in Angus' breathing. As he touched the old man's hand, his eyelids flickered and he managed a gentle return pressure on Dair's hand. Then there was only stillness. The mainstay of his life was gone. Alisdair Munro felt much the way he did on the Liverpool dock in 1937.

CHAPTER 5

Departure

New York to Rome
10 May, 1975

The buzzer sounded at the New York apartment to let Kate know the car to the airport was downstairs. She had planned to leave on the previous night's flight to Rome, but the plane's mechanical trouble had delayed her. Fortunately, Pan Am let her know there was a problem before she left for the airport.

She'd been told her flight would leave at 6 a.m. unless someone called to say otherwise, so now she was anxious to go. She would be arriving much later than she'd planned; almost a full day.

The housekeeper at the apartment had pressed her camel trousers, so she had decided to wear them again. Most of the women on the plane in First Class always wore dresses or suits and high heels.

However, she was going for comfort on this trip, and decided to change only her silk blouse for a linen one to wear under her serviceable brown suede jacket. She kept her walking heels since she didn't plan on actually walking that much. They were easy to slip on and off during the flight if her feet decided to swell.

She was always a light traveler. She had her carry-on, which was good quality and old as the hills. She also had her shoulder bag purse and a small camera bag. She had a larger bag she planned to check through to her hotel. Never pack more than you can carry had always been her motto, and she'd frequently been in situations where she had to do just that. As she aged, toting luggage was less of an adventure and more of a pain.

Fortunately, the doorman and car-service driver were more than happy to schlepp her luggage now. As the doorman waved goodbye, she sank back in the leather seat of the limo and relaxed. She'd had this driver before, and trusted that he would deliver her safely to JFK's Worldport terminal with a minimum of small talk.

After skillfully navigating the congested downtown traffic, the car pulled up in front of the exotic looking Pan Am terminal with its flat, four-acre roof. It was elliptical in shape and eye-catching in the extreme. It befitted the new headquarters of the most popular international carrier in the United States. Pan Am boasted the best pilots as well as flight attendants, who were originally all nurses.

Normally, Kate would have taken the family's private jet, a part of the small fleet of planes the corporation owned. However, Michael had taken their plane somewhere and when she'd decided to make this trip, she didn't have time to track it down. Michael had remained incommunicado, so there had been no check-in from the plane's crew.

Kate exited the car and picked up her purse, then slung the camera bag over her shoulder. She checked the large bag with the outside airline porters and grabbed her carry-on. She was through the doors before anyone could help her, and strolled leisurely down the hallway to the departure gate. She'd been this route enough times to know many of the gate personnel.

After stopping to show her boarding pass, she was greeted by the cabin attendants. Then she was seated and provided with some iced tea, as she scanned the cabin. The arrangement of seating on the planes in First Class varied to some extent. She was glad to see that this plane had a scattered setup, with double seats together against the far side of the plane with single seats scattered on the other side.

There were also tables with four chairs for those who wanted to pass the time with a card game or dining service.

After filling out her menu card, she rifled through her tote bag to find her book, and reclined her seat until takeoff. She had picked up a copy of the new Irving Stone book on the Schliemanns. Jack had been interested in Henry Schliemann's search for the long-lost city of Troy; although he deplored the amateur's sloppy treatment of the long-lost site.

She was more interested in Sophia Schliemann, who had stayed with her single-minded man from her teens to his death 21 years later. She quickly skipped to the center of the book for their breathtaking photos of finding the mythical city.

The photo of Sophia, draped in a shower of jewels from the site, was stunning. This should keep her interested for most of the flight. After a chapter, her interest flagged. She decided she certainly wouldn't have named her son Agamemnon, as they had. Unfortunately, this brought her thoughts back to Michael.

Wherever he was, he wasn't interested in talking with her. That was worrying in itself, because she and Michael were extremely close. He was hiding something. Did it have anything to do with Jack's death? She didn't see how it could, but anything was possible. She was sure he hadn't seen the letter that was responsible for her quick trip to Italy.

While moving from the big house to the coach house, she had cleaned out the contents of Jack's desk. One evening, while the kids were in the Big Apple for dinner and a play, she gathered the hodgepodge of materials. She was dividing things into what to pitch and what to keep.

Most had gone into the pitch pile, but one item had stopped her cold. It was a letter from the niece of the long-time housekeeper to San Sebastiano's priest, Father Tucci. The letter was begging Jack to come to see her while he was in Italy. She wanted him to know something important that her aunt had told her before she died.

The letter indicated that there was doubt in her aunt's mind about the manner in which the priest had died. She didn't think it was an accidental fall. Besides that, the aunt had her suspicions about an American Army officer who had visited the good father on two occasions, one of them being the night the priest died.

Jack was the only American the niece felt she could trust since he'd worked on the church restoration after the war. The letter hinted that the falls that killed both of them had been engineered by someone.

Jack must have been on his way to see her when he had died. Kate didn't like to dwell on that. But he obviously felt compelled to go, even though he hadn't shared the letter or his intentions with her. That was most unusual.

Whatever the reason, she felt she needed to follow up on the letter. His accident had been only a few miles from San Sebastiano. Was that just a coincidence?

She told no one about the contents of the letter. Ted would have told her to forget it. Liz would have insisted someone come with her. Michael, well whatever Michael would have thought, he wasn't around to share it with her.

An hour or so after takeoff, the food carts began to arrive. The individual serving trays were decorated with fresh flowers, fine china and heavy serving utensils on starched white linens. The food was catered using recipes from Maxim's of Paris. Although she had long since gotten used to the luxury surrounding her, she still appreciated the effort.

She was born in New York City in 1925 while her father finished his residency in cardiology at the Cornell University

Hospital. As a second-generation Irish immigrant, he'd had to scramble for an education.

A couple of teaching nuns had seen early promise in their student. They helped him apply for grants and scholarships for his college education, then med school. After that, he got along on sheer talent. Dr. Myles Kelly was one of the East Coast's preeminent cardiologists.

For many years they had lived in Princeton, New Jersey, and Dad would take the train into New York City to operate on patients four days a week. Then he would be home with his wife, Patricia, and the twins. She had one sibling, a twin brother named Mike, who was a bomber pilot in WWII. He was killed leading an attack over Berlin near the end of the war.

That's really how she met Jack. He had returned to Princeton to study under Ernest de Wald, head of the MFAA during the war. One day on the Princeton campus, she was hurrying to meet with De Wald.

She was helping him compile research for a new book on the activities of the Monuments Men. When she opened a door in old McCormick Hall, she literally bumped into Jack Evans. She'd begun to mumble an apology when she looked up and saw his beautiful blue eyes. He was staring at her with a puzzled look.

Later, he told her he could remember her face but it took a minute for him to place her. As she moved to get around him, he finally snapped his fingers and said she had to be Irish Mike's twin sister. Now it was her turn to stare like an idiot. Her instinct had been to ease around this obviously deranged man and go on to her appointment, but she did like his smiling eyes.

When he'd recognized her confusion, he proceeded to tell her about meeting Mike in Italy. Part way through the great story about planning to visit her after the war because of the picture, he'd realized something was very wrong. When he learned of Mike's death, he was sweetly concerned about hurting her.

He'd walked her to De Wald's office, then waited for her to emerge following the appointment. He'd taken her to dinner and they'd continued talking about the war; De Wald; Jack's plans for a career; and her desire to contribute to the world following the devastation of war. They finally left the restaurant at 11:30 because it was closing.

Talk about sweeping me off my feet, she thought. He'd looked at me and I'd looked at him, and something just clicked. They were married six months later. The man who hadn't planned to marry and have kids had finally found a reason to change his mind.

Until they began to plan the wedding, she had little knowledge of who he was in terms of importance and wealth. He was just one of De Wald's ex-Army guys who returned to school on the GI Bill, she thought. An afternoon tea with his mother at their home in New Haven had been enlightening.

She smiled to herself as she remembered both her anger at Jack for not telling her more; and the doubt she felt about becoming part of the Evans clan. Jack solved all that by just holding her and making her a solemn promise. She, and she alone, would make the decisions about what she would and wouldn't do as Mrs. John Evans. And that's how it had worked.

His mother had not approved of their gypsy lives as they moved around from dig to dig in their summers, but she had never tried to interfere. Kate assumed that was because Jack had also laid down the rules for her, as well.

In actual fact, Kate had liked her mother-in-law very much. That woman could have made her life much more difficult, but she'd paved the way for Kate to move into society with little difficulty. Kate hoped that she would be equally welcoming for whomever Michael decided to marry.

When they moved to Yale after Jack finished his Ph.D., they lived in a smaller home near campus in Hamden. Once the twins were born, they found a much bigger house in an elegant area on Whitney Avenue.

When Jack planned an archeological dig, he always found nice quarters for her and the twins. Hugh was often part of those expeditions in the initial stages, making sure all the items they needed for their stay were procured and shipped.

Carlo always took very good care of them, as well, especially if the dig was in Italy. It often seemed that Carlo had either friends or relatives in every Italian city and town. The twins still referred to him as Tio Carlo.

When it came to participating in the New York social scene, she could again choose what to do or not do. She was a partner when they set up the Kelly-Evans Foundation. She reveled in the philanthropic side of her life, especially when so many of their projects were hand-picked by her.

She also learned to be comfortable as Mrs. John Evans, the charming hostess, committee chair and dinner companion. Eventually, she also learned how to avoid those who thought she might be an easy mark for a sad story. Jack had taught her to be tough in dealing with those who thought to take advantage of a newcomer to New York society.

Life had been perfect until he'd left for that quick business trip to Naples in 1970. The fact that San Sebastiano was so close to Naples had provided the perfect opportunity for a side trip.

Her perfect life ended with a phone call from the president of the company Jack had been there to meet. Details came in next from the American Embassy. As life shattered around her, she'd had to draw on reserves to help others. Michael was in the Army and Liz was planning her wedding.

It had taken her a while to find her feet after his death. He had been the center of her life for more than 22 years. For about a year, she'd made few important decisions. She was now the Chairman of the Board and the major shareholder of the Evans Corporation. However, the corporation was composed of a dozen companies operated by presidents who knew what they were doing and needed little oversight.

Ted Sanders had taken over most of the decisions for the Foundation. He'd kept things on an even keel until she'd felt ready to rejoin everyday life. She had been so grateful to him and had helped him grieve when his wife, Estelle, had drowned.

Gradually, she'd started working on art history projects and writing articles for publication in her spare time. She usually did her own photography, as well. Her reputation was growing in the art community for not only being a knowledgeable collector, but also for her willingness to work with museums wanting to acquire or sell collections.

She particularly liked to help women artists when she could. She felt they were sadly underrepresented in most museums.

All this past history came rolling back as she thought about her family and the different paths they were following. Liz and her husband seemed settled, getting ready for the joys and woes of parenthood. She knew Jonathan loved Liz deeply. They were a good match. Jonathan had no idea who the Evans family was until he proposed, and then he didn't care.

The thought of all the wealth and responsibility that Liz would inherit might have scared off a lesser man, but Jonathan, wrapped up in his physics problems, never blinked. He thought that whatever Liz wanted was just fine with him. He was a good man.

Michael was a different story. He'd been severely wounded when he left Viet Nam and the men in his company behind. Recovery had taken months, and the physical wounds had healed well. He'd spent endless hours in rehab and later in physical training.

It was the mental wounds she worried about. He would not discuss his time in Viet Nam, nor what was bothering him. He was now the vice-chairman of the Evans Corporation, but he had yet to set a foot in the office. He knew she was a good administrator and had no problem with the direction things were going.

She continued to be the family representative at public events. Someday soon Michael and Liz would decide what the future would hold. If they decided to break up the corporation and sell, she would support their decision.

As the lights began to come up around the cabin, attendants brought out a light meal to tide passengers over until dinner time. People began to gather up books, papers and magazines; fill carry-on bags; and get ready for landing.

The touchdown in the big jet was relatively smooth with only one slight hop before settling to taxi across the tarmac to the Leonardo da Vinci Airport south of Rome. A car had been hired to pick her up and take her to the lovely old hotel where she often stayed. She stretched as she stood, then picked up her bags for a quick departure.

Carlo had arranged the local car hire, undoubtedly owned by one of his relatives. After clearing customs with only a few perfunctory questions and making sure her checked bag would be forwarded to the hotel, she headed down the exit hallway toward ground transportation. As she glanced at her watch, she saw that it would be getting dark very soon.

CHAPTER 6

Kidnapped

Rome Airport
10 May 1975

Kate was looking for a driver holding a sign, never realizing she was being closely monitored by at least three pairs of interested eyes. Dair Munro was stationed outside the customs door, waiting to relay her position to Quinn O'Malley, who was outside with a car.

Another pair of eyes was looking for the woman whose picture he held, along with a sign with her name. He was to be her driver. The third pair was hidden behind large sunglasses and positioned under an awning stretched over a newsvendor's stand.

As the departure crowd thinned around her, Kate finally saw the sign with her name. She hadn't known whether Carlo had planned to pick her up or someone from the hotel had been assigned to fetch her. Since she didn't recognize the sign holder, he must have been sent by the hotel. It was too bad, since Kate had looked forward to reuniting with Carlo, if only for one night.

The driver had now seen her and was stepping forward to greet her. "Buonosera, Signora Evans. I'm Luigi, your driver. May I help you with your luggage?"

Kate smiled and handed him her larger bag. He grabbed it and said, "Please follow me, Signora. My car is right out front." He then proceeded to set a fast pace as he plowed through the remaining passengers.

He led her to a late model Mercedes-Benz parked near the exit doors. He opened the rear door and got her settled inside, then closed her bag in the trunk before slipping into the driver's seat. With a minimum of honking, gesturing and yelling on the part of waiting taxi drivers, the car pulled away from the curb.

In the meantime, Dair had also exited the building and was getting in the passenger seat of the waiting Fiat as the Benz pulled away. "This guy isn't wasting any time, Quinn, so don't lose him in traffic."

"Don't worry," Quinn said. "It's a half hour drive into Rome, so we should be able to settle in behind him before we hit city traffic. The Cavalieri Hotel is in the Montemario sector, so we can always cut around them and then let them pass us."

As she sat back to enjoy the scenery on the drive into Rome, Kate asked, "Do you have any water, Luigi? I didn't take time to get anything at the airport and plane travel always makes me thirsty."

"Si, Signora, if you lift the lid on the chest beside you, there are bottles of Perrier," he said. "I would have had a bottle waiting for you, but I didn't know if it would get too warm while I waited. I know you like your water cooled."

Well, Kate thought, the hotel certainly had her preferences pegged. She followed the driver's instructions and found two or three bottles cooling in ice. There were also glasses on a shelf attached to the chest.

She opened and poured the water, taking a healthy swallow as she sat back. She continued to watch out the window, sipping her water, until her eyes closed and her head fell back against the seat. The water glass fell to the carpeted floor while Kate lost consciousness.

Behind the Benz, Quinn and Dair kept a careful watch on the car, pacing it but not getting too close. They were still several miles from the city when the driver ahead took an unexpected exit from the highway.

"What the hell is this all about?" Dair said. "This isn't a shortcut to the hotel. It doesn't even go directly to Rome."

Meanwhile, Quinn was busy making hasty lane changes and getting some Italian curses hurled at him. He managed to make the exit the Benz had taken. The black car was some distance ahead when they finally saw it. Quinn put his foot down in an effort to cut the distance.

"I hope this doesn't become a road race," he said. "This Fiat is no competition for the Benz."

Dair was busy trying to keep track of the car ahead and saw its brake lights come on long enough to slow for a quick right turn.

"Maybe being further back is OK for now. At least when we make the turn, he may be far enough ahead not to notice us. That might keep his speed down," Dair said.

"Yeah, maybe," Quinn answered. "I wish we had brought a couple more cars in on this detail. I don't think any of us expected her to go anywhere but the hotel. Does this mean she expected to be tailed? That wouldn't look very good for her. Maybe she's not as innocent as we thought."

"True," Dair said, "but maybe that driver wasn't sent by the hotel. I'm going to call Inspector Russo and have him check with the hotel. Something about this doesn't add up."

Reaching for the car radio, he asked to be put through to the inspector and relayed his request. Five minutes later, Russo returned his call.

"Inspector Munro, the Hotel Cavalieri tells me that the car they had scheduled for Mrs. Evans was cancelled earlier today. They were also told not to expect her to arrive until tomorrow. What would you like us to do?"

Dair frowned, then responded. "Let's see if we can find where they go, and then I'll call you back. This whole thing is way off-plan right now. Thanks."

"I'll stand by to hear from you," Russo said and hung up.

Quinn had continued to follow the black car as closely as possible while not giving away the fact it was being followed. Fortunately, tan Fiats were as common as grass in the Italian countryside, so the driver would have to be looking very closely to know he was being followed.

About 20 minutes later, the car ahead slowed and turned down a dusty lane. The Interpol car stopped at the head of the lane, not anxious to kick up any dust that the driver ahead could see in his rearview mirror. "What now?" Quinn said.

"Do you have any idea where we are?" asked Dair, searching the glove box for a map of the area.

"I think we're somewhere south of Rome, about 20 miles out," Quinn said. "We need the name of a village if you can find one."

"OK, I think the dust has settled a bit," Dair said, still scanning the map in his lap. "Why don't you try the road, driving very slowly. Let's see if there is a farm or house or something up here."

Ten minutes earlier, Luigi had pulled the Benz into the yard of a small farmhouse. He went to the door and knocked. It was opened by an old Italian woman who stood silently while he entered.

"Is everything ready, Grandmother?" Luigi asked. The woman nodded and led him through the kitchen to a small bedroom. A length of rope lay curled on the floor and a tattered shade covered the window to the sill.

"The Reverend Father will be pleased," he told her.

Returning to the car, he opened the rear door and roughly pulled the unconscious woman out. Hoisting her on his shoulder, he carried her through to the bedroom where he dumped her unconscious body on the dirty bed.

He picked up the rope and made quick work of tying her hands and ankles. He also stuffed a handkerchief in her mouth as a final touch. Then he returned to the car and brought in her luggage and purse, dumping them in one corner.

He made sure the car revealed no trace of the American woman other than the bottle and glass. He removed both of them and dumped them in a trash barrel beside the house. Looking around, he decided his work was finished and he made for the back door.

"This is a bad woman, Grandmother," he said. "Don't untie her, no matter what she says. She is a devil from America who wants to hurt the Holy Father. Keep her quiet and don't let anyone near her. You will be blessed."

Nodding her compliance, the old woman closed and locked the door behind him. He once again got into the Benz and slowly backed out of the drive. The dust from his departure was just beginning to settle when the Interpol car crept down the lane.

"Do you think that was our Benz?" Dair asked.

Quinn just shrugged. "Maybe."

"If it was, they should have been much further down the road unless they stopped somewhere, maybe this farmhouse," he pointed.

"That's a lot of maybes," Quinn said, "but you're right. We were about 10 minutes behind him. If that was him, he must have stopped somewhere along here. What do you think?"

His finger was pointing straight at the old farmhouse that had appeared at the side of the lane. As he stopped, Dair exited the car and walked carefully into the yard. Some vehicle had disturbed the dust recently, and a small spot of fresh oil decorated the grass.

Then his eye was caught by a pair of sunglasses that had dropped next to the rickety porch. They were very expensive sunglasses, much like a wealthy American woman might choose. It wasn't proof, but it might justify a knock on the door.

Gesturing to Quinn, he walked to the door and knocked. Quinn had pulled into the yard and got out to walk around the house. No one came to the door. He knocked again and heard someone move stealthily. He tried knocking again and finally the door cracked open enough for him to see the old woman in a long, dingy dress. With her straggly grey hair and wrinkled skin, she did not look like someone who would be part of an international art-theft ring.

He smiled and said in his best Italian, "Good evening, Signora, I'm looking for a friend of mine who invited me to stay at her home. It's supposed to be somewhere in this area. Do you know if there are any large homes in the area? I seem to be lost."

The old woman looked at him dumbly and started shaking her head. No, no one with a large home. She knew nothing. "Go away, go away." And firmly slammed the door.

Quinn came around the house and walked over. "This is just a rundown wreck of a house. There's no upstairs, just the one floor. There is some kind of room in the back with a window. It's covered with a window shade," he said.

"Interesting, could you see anything inside?" Dair asked.

"Not really, it's sagging, so there is a little bit of visibility on one side. All I could see was a bit of bed and what looked like a piece of rope. Not exactly like what you'd expect to see in a bedroom," he added.

Dair was more puzzled than ever. What had started out as a sting to find stolen art work was beginning to look like something very different. He decided to have a look around the house, as well, and stopped at the barrel.

"You know," he said, "that old woman did not strike me as the Perrier water type. And I'd be willing to bet that house doesn't have any glassware of this caliber. If she had a glass like this, she'd never throw it in the trash. I think I need to call Russo again."

Using the car radio, he got in touch with the inspector again, gave directions to the farm, and was promised that someone from the Italian Carabinieri would join him as soon as possible.

Roman police took care of city offences and the countryside was under the auspices of the Carabinieri. Woe to the city police who did not respect that difference, Dair thought.

He had had the occasional encounter with the Carabinieri, but it had usually been in a cooperative effort with the higher-ups concerning criminal arrests. He wasn't sure how happy the more garden-variety officer was going to be about Interpol agents wandering around bothering little old Italian ladies.

Almost half an hour later, an official police car pulled into the driveway and a pair of officers got out. They were wearing aviator style sunglasses and no smiles.

They waited for Dair and Quinn to approach them. In short order, Dair explained what had happened at the airport, the fact that the hotel had not sent a car, and the deviation of the Benz from the road to Rome. He ended by showing the men the Perrier bottle, the glass and then the sunglasses. At this point, he fudged a bit and told them he had seen Mrs. Evans wearing the sunglasses when she got in the car.

It appeared the Carabinieri were not impressed. Finally, one of them stepped to the door and knocked. Again, there was no answer. Again, the officer knocked. Still no answer. Now, the officer looked a bit steamed. His knock was louder the third time and he loudly announced "Polizia." The door opened slightly. He shoved it open wider and began to enter when a gunshot roared inside.

The officer was down and bleeding. His partner, once he came out of shock, raced to the door, crouched and knocked it open enough for him to see the old woman on the floor. She had used a rusty old shotgun that had exploded as she pulled the trigger.

Dair had reached the injured officer and was attempting to stop the bleeding when the other Carabinieri returned from looking at the rest of the house. He ran to the patrol car and reported the need for backup and an ambulance.

Then he returned to Dair and said, "That old gun was a relic. It probably hadn't been fired in 40 years. She's alive but just barely. I doubt you'll ever be able to talk to her."

That was probably more words than he used in the past week. It was a lot of information, with the last part being of particular interest to Dair.

"Is it all right if I go check on the bedroom?" he asked.

"I don't want you tramping through the mess in the kitchen. Our officers will want the crime scene untouched," the Carabinieri said. Relenting somewhat, he said, "It looks like there's something on the bed. If you can get in through the back window, that shouldn't interfere with our evidence out here."

Dair and Quinn hurried around the house to the window and tried to jimmy it open. Painted shut, it had obviously not been opened in the past three decades.

Finally, Quinn found a good-sized rock and used it to break the glass. Clearing out the glass shards, Dair put his raincoat over the sill and climbed in. Whoever was on the bed never moved. He told Quinn to wait outside, since he'd never get his shoulders through the window, then he turned to the bed.

The figure was still as death. It was now fully dark and he could feel the ropes but couldn't see to cut them.

"Have we got a flashlight in the car?" he asked Quinn. Moments later, Quinn was back with a large light that he shone inside the room. Now Quinn could see the woman on the bed. He removed the gag from her mouth and began to work at the knots on her wrists. She was deeply unconscious and showed no sign of waking.

Dair freed her wrists and ankles, then turned to Quinn. "We need to get her out of here and to someplace where we can have her checked by a doctor. They must have given her a really big dose of the knockout drug. I'm going to pass her through the window to you, then I'll go tell the officer we're leaving. I'm sure he's going to be thrilled, but I'll let him know I'll be at his headquarters tomorrow to give my statement. They'll be wanting a witness that they did nothing wrong to precipitate the gunfire."

Picking Kate up, he turned her carefully so that Quinn could get his arms first under her shoulders and then under her legs. Then Dair was out the window and around the house to open the rear doors of the Fiat.

He got in on the off-side while Quinn slip Kate across to him. They turned her on her side so that her back was pressed against the seat to ease her breathing. Then he left to severely irritate the remaining officer. Fortunately, another Carabinieri car arrived and after a short delay, verifying credentials and exchanging addresses, they were allowed to take Kate away.

CHAPTER 7

Carlo

That Night in Rome
10 May 1975

Michael moved quietly through the old alleys of Rome. He'd returned to Italy only that afternoon, and his jet lag was clouding his senses. He'd come a long way from Asia in a very short time, so he badly needed sleep and something to eat.

He'd been on the move nonstop for three weeks. When he'd reached New York yesterday and called home, it was to hear from his sister that their mother had left for Italy. No wonder he had a nagging headache. He'd called her hotel, but was told she was not in at the moment. He'd left a message, but thought he might get lucky and find her at Tio Carlo's.

Guiding him were memories of the old days in Rome when he and Liz had wandered the ancient streets of the city. He wound through the rabbit's warren of old apartment buildings on streets paved with irregularly laid stones. He stopped letting his mind roam and paused for a minute to decide on the best approach to Tio Carlo's apartment. He badly wanted to get the older man's take on what was going on; but until he reunited with his mother, he didn't want to attract attention.

Carlo Bernini had been an urchin roaming the streets of Rome during WWII. He'd managed to snatch a rudimentary education from the good Sisters of St. Lucy Filippini. They had not only taught the children of Rome during the day, but at night had been guardians to more than 100 Jewish guests sheltered in their convents.

Carlo had taken great pleasure in helping to feed these people by stealing food from the Nazi commissaries every night. He and his friends had thrown rocks at the German soldiers as they boarded trucks to evacuate the city.

When the Nazis left, he continued scrounging, this time from the American food supply, to feed his friends and the nuns. The Americans seemed to have an unlimited supply of food; at least to a youngster who'd made do on the edge of starvation for six years.

By the time Jack Evans had come to Rome to find workers for a dig near Herculaneum, Carlo was a strong young 20-year-old with a desire to rise in the world. He'd started to work as a digger, found it interesting, and proceeded to learn on-the-job all he could from Jack about archeology. They made a good team.

Carlo had friends and relatives by the score to call on for projects Jack developed in Italy. When they started working outside Europe, he took on more responsibility. He could find whatever Jack needed wherever they went. He also picked up a smattering of other languages and could recognize a kindred spirit wherever they went. He could also smell a villain a mile away, so Jack never ended up hiring troublemakers.

When Jack married Kate and they started a family, Carlo was the go-to guy. He could find a house for Kate, keep an eye on the twins, and locate an experienced crew for Jack like nobody else in the business. It was no wonder the twins quickly honored him with the title Tio, or uncle, as soon as they could talk.

Their last project together had been the summer of 1968 on a dig in Jordan. Michael had talked with both Carlo and Jack about joining the Army before he was drafted. They had both been opposed.

What neither man said, but Michael understood, was that they couldn't bear to think that he might be injured or killed in some distant jungle. Seven years later, Lt. Michael Evans had been seriously injured; Jack Evans was dead; and Carlo Bernini had retired.

Michael stopped thinking about the past and realized he was near the apartment off the Piazza Margutta. It was late, and in this area, there were few people on the streets with whom to mingle. Solitary male pedestrians would attract attention from anyone watching Tio Carlo's home, and, until he knew otherwise, he would assume someone was watching.

Carlo had managed to get a message to him as he was steaming his way toward Manilla. While they were still two days out of port, the ship's captain had brought him a cablegram. Carlo let him know that he'd found some of the San Sebastiano relatives of the old housekeeper and her niece. The dead girl had confided in them. She had talked with her aunt at some length and had gotten a very good description of the man her aunt thought had murdered the priest, along with the name he used.

He had worn an American Army uniform and called himself Captain Milo Constantine. From the description, he had an idea who that might be. He'd ended the cable with that identity unshared. Michael was concerned. Had Carlo taken precautions? That knowledge was clearly a powder keg.

Michael moved as quietly as possible to the rear of the old building that housed Carlo's second-floor apartment. There was a balcony overhanging the lower floor. Fortunately, the downstairs neighbor had built a wooden enclosure for the trash barrel. Standing atop that, Michael was able to pull himself onto the balcony and peer through the closed curtain.

He was unable to see anything; no light, no movement, no Carlo. He gently touched the door handle and was surprised to find it open. Carlo was a careful man who had lived life on the edge since childhood. He didn't leave doors unlocked, whether he was home or not. Pushing it gently to the side, he prayed that it wouldn't squeak. If Carlo heard him at the door, he'd be waiting inside with a baseball bat.

"Tio Carlo?" he said quietly. There was no reply, but Carlo would have known it was Michael had he been inside. He cautiously stepped over the sill, pushing the soft drape aside. Then he froze.

The smell attacking his nose was familiar, and not good. The odors of blood and feces were pungent. He pulled a small, hooded flashlight from his pocket and slowly scanned the floor. There was an overturned lamp, a broken chair leg, and finally, beside the old sofa, there was Carlo.

He'd been badly beaten and was obviously dead. Blood was splattered in several directions; and his bowels had emptied as he died. The beating had been severe, but it was the jagged cut to his throat that had killed him.

Michael had seen violent death many times, but this one struck like a physical blow. Whoever had killed Carlo had enjoyed his work. Michael tried to be dispassionate as he examined the scene. The blood on the walls and furniture was nearly dry, but the pool under Carlo's head was still a bit damp. In spite of the warmth in the room, there weren't many flies yet. So, death was probably this morning sometime.

This had taken time. Why? As he straightened, he was sure this had something to do with the cablegram and the investigating Carlo had been doing. He had hoped to find his mother here with Carlo. Liz had thought Mom was coming to see Carlo. She'd even made arrangements for Carlo to pick her up at the airport. Where was she now? Had Carlo said anything to her about his investigations? Was she in danger, as well?

Retracing his steps, Michael was back on the balcony before he realized there were probably people watching the apartment, knowing someone from the Evans family was likely to come here sooner or later. He crouched, making as small a target as possible. He'd worn dark clothing for his midnight stroll, but he was armed only with the knife he perpetually carried in his boot.

He spent 15 long minutes on the balcony, using his Ranger training to scan the backyards that abutted the apartment; ardently wishing he had some night goggles. He knew some of Carlo's sisters lived within a block of this apartment, so he felt no compunction about leaving the scene without reporting it. Someone would discover him soon.

He saw no movement, not even the flap of laundry on the lines, but he did have the feeling something was off. That feeling had saved his life a time or two in Viet Nam. This murder had happened some hours ago; so, surveillance may have been abandoned.

Very slowly, he extended first one leg and then the other toward the waiting trash bin, then leapt agilely to the ground and again crouched. Nothing. He quickly exited the yard, staying as close to the building as possible. He returned the way he had come, in case whoever was watching the apartment was stupid enough to watch only the front door.

Then he walked hurriedly away. Don't run, don't call attention to yourself! Where to now? He needed a quiet place to think.

Then he had an idea. He hadn't seen her in years, but he knew Tata, his old Italian nanny, would open the door wide when she realized it was her little Michelino. She had cared for Michael and Liz during the two summers their parents had been involved with the dig at Herculaneum.

They had grown very close and leaving her behind when they ventured into the Middle East had been a wrench, but they had needed a caretaker who could speak the local language.

He had talked to her by phone the summer after his dad died, but he hadn't seen her in eight or nine years. He didn't want to endanger her, but he was sure no one would know where he was as long as he wasn't followed to her house. More importantly, if he could contact his mother through Liz, she would know where to find him.

Circling around to the other side of the piazza, he grabbed a tram two blocks down for a trip to the southern suburbs.

CHAPTER 8

Explanation

Next Day in Rome
11 May 1975

When Kate opened her eyes, she immediately regretted it. Excruciating pain shot through her head, caused by the light pouring through a nearby window. The second time she tried, it still hurt, but if she just squinted, she could see that she lay on a small bed with a blanket over her.

On her third try, some minutes later, she realized she wasn't in her suite at the Hotel Cavalieri. She was in a room about the size of her closet at home. It held the bed, a small table with an ugly lamp, and a wooden armchair holding a slumped, rumpled man with his eyes closed. He did not look comfortable.

Vaguely she remembered the airport and the car. That prodded her mind to wonder how she'd gotten from the car's back seat to a bed in this room. Then there was the presence of an unknown man. Fighting the remaining pain, she lifted her head and the man stirred.

"Hello," he said softly, moving toward her. "Mrs. Evans, I mean you no harm. You're currently in an Interpol safe house. I have a lot of explaining to do, and I'm sure this is going to be confusing for you. First though, would you like something to drink? You must be very thirsty."

She continued to assess him, and finally decided he didn't seem to be an immediate threat. He *had* slept in the chair. She decided she wasn't up to nodding, and limited her answer to a raspy 'yes'. He rose quickly and went to the table where water and glasses sat waiting. After pouring the water, he crossed the room to help her sit up. As she swallowed, she could see his face much better.

He had laugh-lines around his grey eyes; his silver-streaked black hair fell forward over a small scar on his forehead; and his hands were clean and well-shaped as he assisted her with the glass.

There was a soft burr to his voice, which indicated he was from one of the Celtic parts of the world. On the whole, he looked somewhat trustworthy.

"Was there an accident with the car?" she asked. She had no memory of a crash, but that was the most sensible explanation for her present situation.

"No, Mrs. Evans, there was no accident," he answered. "I'm afraid the real cause of your being here is going to seem very bizarre. I'm Alisdair Munro, an Interpol investigator. My partner, Quinn O'Malley, is sitting out in the hall right now keeping an eye on things while we talk."

"Talk about what?" Kate asked, giving him much closer scrutiny than before. "May I see some identification?"

Pulling a wallet from his suit jacket, he handed it to her. She gave it a thorough examination; flipped through the photo and Interpol ID information; then handed it back.

"All right. I've never seen an Interpol ID before, but I'll accept it for now. Please explain," she said, gesturing to the room.

"This is going to take a while and you're going to have a lot of questions, but bear with me and I'll tell you as much as I can. First, you are in this room because the driver of the car that picked you up at the airport drugged you. He wasn't sent by the hotel, but by someone who wanted to kidnap you.

My partner and I followed the car, discovered where you had been taken, and worked with the Carabinieri to rescue you."

Kate stared at him, now in some doubt as to his mental stability. It sounded like a novel; pure fiction. Why had they been following her in the first place?

Dair watched her face as she worked through the story then hastened to add, "I know this sounds unbelievable, but one of the Carabinieri officers was seriously injured and may die because he was the first to open the door to the house where you were being held. An old woman who lived there died as a result of an explosion. If you look at your wrists and ankles, you'll see the abrasions from the ropes that bound you."

Kate glanced at her wrists and saw some fading red marks. After a pause, she said, "Go on."

"All this goes back 30 years, to WWII, and a lot of missing artworks," he said. "About four years ago, in 1971, Interpol got a call from a young curator at a small museum in Lyons, France, about a painting. Although it was obviously of high quality and probably genuine, he could not find out exactly how the museum had acquired it.

"He wanted to know if it was possible that it was part of the looted Nazi art. Right now, there is no comprehensive list of missing artworks from the era. Most of the lists are bits and pieces compiled by the former countries that discovered the looted art."

Dair could see she was following the convoluted story with intense concentration.

"By comparing those," he said, "we came up with names of still missing paintings. But those are by no means complete. Some countries have been more rigorous in their pursuit of these artifacts, and others would prefer to remain ignorant of what is still missing. Since so much was looted and so much was destroyed by either the Nazis or the Allied bombing, we're still trying to take things case by case.

"We've been dealing with this sort of thing since 1949, but when this curator told us the name of the painting and the artist, we were surprised. It was listed as the 1508 rendering of the *Assumption of the Virgin* by Fra Bartolomeo. This painting wasn't on any list of missing art treasures. It took a while for us to finally put the pieces together but eventually we discovered that the painting wasn't on lists because it wasn't supposed to exist."

Kate asked, "It was a forgery?"

"No, it was genuine all right," Dair said. "But it was one of several great works that were supposedly burned in 1945 when the Allies bombed Dresden. This was our first hint that at least some of those paintings might have survived.

"Further investigation told us that it had been donated to the museum by an Italian Contessa who has since died. Interpol talked with her family, but none of them admitted to knowing anything about the painting. They said it wasn't in the inventory of family works. We checked the rest of their holdings, but there was nothing like what we were seeking."

He paused to pour more water for her, which she gratefully accepted, and continued his story.

"We decided it must have been a clerical error when the lists were compiled, but we kept the file open. The next time a curator called, it rang very large alarm bells. This was in 1973. The painting was a Caravaggio, *Portrait of a Courtesan,* painted around 1597. It was listed as destroyed by fire in the Frederikshavn Flakturm, following the capture of Berlin in May of 1945.

"Hundreds of paintings had been stored in this watchtower because it was thought to be impregnable. But the fire was started inside, by workmen repairing the tower. This curator's call was beyond coincidence and wasn't something anyone could ignore, so a special unit was formed at Interpol to find out if more of these supposedly destroyed artworks existed and who had them.

"The Caravaggio was in a private collection, but the owner wanted to donate it to a museum and take a tax write-off. The museum was thrilled until the curator realized what he was being offered."

Kate said, "I can imagine. We've been fortunate enough to be able to donate some artworks ourselves. It was something my husband really believed in, and he enjoyed finding a piece that would fit the needs of a specific museum."

"Yes, well, I'm coming to that shortly," Dair said. He shifted in his chair uncomfortably and went on with his story.

"We sent out the names and artists of the remaining paintings thought lost in Dresden and Berlin to all the museum directors in Europe and North America. There were nearly 100 of the very best of their genre. We were more discreet about sending the warning to South American museums since we already knew that some of the German loot had landed there and been gratefully accepted by collectors."

Kate was intrigued by the story, but she didn't know how this affected her. "I don't see where I come into this. This can't have anything to do with why I was drugged, can it?" she asked.

"Just be patient. There's a story here that's going to be hard for you to believe and you need the background," Dair said.

"OK, we've got major artwork that shouldn't exist showing up. The guy looking to donate the painting was subjected to intense investigation, but it looked like he'd just been used by a third party.

"He'd found the painting in a small gallery in Pisa where he was assured it was being sold by an Italian aristocrat who needed money. Most Italian aristocrats after the war were selling things to keep afloat. He'd had the piece for 15 years and was ready to pare down his collection, especially if he could get a hefty tax credit."

Kate was getting fidgety. She had a feeling she wasn't going to like where this was going, but she couldn't understand the situation yet.

"About this time, we connected the dots on how the paintings had survived. Fortunately for us, the Germans kept meticulous records of everything, even the secret transactions. We sent someone to Berlin to start digging through rooms of files looking for anything mentioning the paintings we were targeting. There were some really unbelievable titles and artist names on the list.

"He eventually found an inventory of about 20 of the missing paintings with a notation that these had been sent to Paris by the SS at Hitler's personal command. This inventory was buried in a file of papers belonging to a Colonel Werner Lang, who was one of Hitler's principal aides.

"It took Interpol's agent five months to find it, but it was worth it. Also in the file was a memorandum that these would be transported to a place called San Sebastiano al Vesuvio for receipt by Benito Mussolini."

Now he had Kate's full attention. San Sebastiano had been part of her family's story since she married Jack.

"San Sebastiano al Vesuvio is a little town near Naples, that was destroyed by the 1944 eruption of Mt. Vesuvius," he went on. "Why Hitler would be sending something there for Mussolini was a huge question, but when we looked through Mussolini's background information, we found what we thought was a connection.

"He wasn't religious unless it served his purpose for attracting supporters. However, his mother was a devout Catholic and so was her mother - who had lived in San Sebastiano. We finally found evidence that Mussolini's mother had him baptized there on a visit to grandma. The church was his only tie to the town."

Kate sat silently as she digested this. Jack had told her about his trip there and his meeting with the little priest. He'd liked the man so much that he'd gone back a few months later with a small crew to excavate the church before he came home. He said the people of the town had already decided to rebuild it and he admired them for their determination.

His crew wasn't large enough to do much shifting of the debris, but the locals helped. They got it cleaned up enough he could find some smaller statues and the most recent parish records, which hadn't been stored in the rectory.

Jack had made sure the rebuilding of the church got a hefty donation from their Foundation. She looked at Dair, then decided to share the story with him.

"We checked the church next, of course. The priest your husband knew, Father Tucci, was dead. The new chap had arrived after the reconstruction. Some of the locals remembered helping your husband with the digging. His main local assistant told us that he had dug down around the altar area, but they didn't try to move it to look in the crypt. They'd found what the priest was interested in and he didn't want the bodies of his predecessors disturbed. That's what we were told.

"Later, however, when the architects working on the reconstruction opened the crypt to check the foundations, they'd found more bodies than they expected. There were five soldiers in American uniforms lying near the stairs beside several open cannisters. The bodies had no dog tags, so they weren't sure how to identify them. Their remains had been mummified, what with the perfect temperature and humidity in the crypt," he explained.

"Working with American military officials, we found that they had no records of missing soldiers from that area at that time. Because of the destruction, it was obvious the bodies had been put there in 1944, before March 20.

"There had been American soldiers in the area for the preceding 16 months, but not so many that they could lose five without knowing it. Especially since these men had been shot in the head, execution-style," he added meaningfully.

There was silence in the room as Kate's eyes met his. She was having trouble reading him as he looked at her, then glanced away. He began to speak again. By now she was sitting upright with her feet on the floor, as if poised to run. She was very uncomfortable with the way this story was unfolding.

"We decided that they must have been part of the crew sent with the paintings to San Sebastiano. They had been eliminated as witnesses. I know its speculation, but it fits the evidence too well."

Kate moistened her dry lips, then said, "If I understand, you're saying that priceless works of art were taken from two German museums, reported burned so that no one would be looking for them; then transported to Italy in some kind of deal with Mussolini?"

"Yes," Dair said.

"You're also saying that the paintings were stored in the crypt of a church that my husband worked on shortly after they were put there. Now those paintings are appearing again on the open market. Let me guess, you're thinking that he may have opened that crypt, found the paintings and then sold them after the war. Right?"

She was on her feet, furious and ready to do battle.

"Jack Evans would never have done anything like that. He was the most honorable man I ever met. He also had too much respect for art objects to treat them in such an underhanded way. If he'd found them, he would have announced it joyfully to the whole world. You're all idiots!

"Why would he steal something like that when he inherited a fortune so massive, he could buy whatever painting he wanted. And, he gave a good deal of that fortune to charity and museums around the world," she said.

She was just getting warmed up when Dair held up both hands to stop her.

"Just hold on. We came to the same conclusion. I'm afraid the truth is going to be much harder for you to hear. We don't think his death was an accident; we think he was murdered. We're guessing he became suspicious for some reason and was going to San Sebastiano to find out what was going on," Dair said.

Kate's anger left her as she digested this information. Murdered? Jack? She shook her head slowly back and forth, totally deflated. That had come out of left field and left her helpless. Someone had cut short that wonderful man's life? No, no, her mind protested.

"Sit down and have some of this. There's more I have to tell you when you feel ready," Dair said as he offered her a glass half filled with something that didn't look like plain water. Whiskey had never been her drink of choice, but right now she was not going to be picky.

"What more do you know?" she asked.

Dair helped her to sit on the bed and took his seat in the chair facing her. "The truth is, four more of the paintings have surfaced since we put out the alert. Most of them are in museums in the United States and at least three of them were donated by the same family. We're still trying to pin down the origin of the fourth one. Care to guess the name of the family?" Dair asked.

Kate didn't have to work too hard to figure out he meant the Evans family. "Us?" she ventured quietly.

The expression on Dair's face told her she'd guessed right.

"Explain, please," she said

"Since he's the one who was interested in purchasing and donating artwork, Jack's was the name on the contributor's list for three of the paintings. We think he got suspicious when one of the curators at the National Gallery asked him about the provenance of the last painting he donated.

"That would have been just before he went on that last trip. If he thought there was a problem, don't you think he would have started asking questions?" Dair asked.

"I can't believe he wouldn't have talked to me about it," she insisted. "We always made our decisions jointly – about what we would buy and donate. Of course, most of that process was Jack's, but he always asked my opinion."

Dair turned that over in his mind for a while, then said, "Do you know if he bought all three paintings from the same place?"

"No, I don't," Kate said. "I don't think so, but the Foundation actually paid for the paintings and I was more involved with deciding if I liked the subject matter and artist. Of course, if it was a really well-known artist, I usually rubber-stamped his find because we were always excited about sharing the great works with the public."

Dair was pleased to hear that Kate hadn't been involved with the purchases. What she didn't realize yet was that if Jack had been killed to keep the thief's secret, the thief would kill again – anyone whom he felt threatened him.

"There's something you don't know," Kate said. "It's the reason Jack was headed for San Sebastiano when he died. He'd received a letter from the niece of Father Tucci's housekeeper. Apparently, her aunt had told her there was something wrong with the fall the father took. She hadn't spoken to anyone after Father Tucci died, because she thought he was murdered by Americans.

"I don't have any idea why she would have thought that. That's one of the things that drove me to make this trip. I want to talk with the niece if I can find her. According to her letter, she lives in Rome, at 22 Via Giulia."

Dair made a note of the address and returned his attention to Kate.

"The Foundation would be a good place to start looking," Kate mused. "We can check the purchase records and I'll speak to Ted Sanders about what he knows. Jack also had a man who did a lot of the actual locating of the paintings. His name is Milo Constantine. He knows the dealers and collectors, particularly in Europe. He was always involved when art was on Jack's mind. I think his headquarters are here in Rome."

Then she added, "Of course, when we find Michael, we can ask him, too. If there's anyone who knows where Jack bought things, it would be Michael. He is not only Jack's son, but also his dad's top field assistant. Except for the months he was in school, he was always with Jack. And Jack always set up his field digs so they coincided with the time Michael was free, or could study with a tutor rather than in a classroom."

At that point, the import of what she'd just said hit her. Jack was dead, probably because of what he knew. If he had shared that information with his son, was the thief looking to tie up all the loose ends by killing the entire Evans family? Was that why she'd been drugged and kidnapped? Was that why Michael was missing? Was Liz safe, even in New Haven?

"We really need to find Michael and I need to make some phone calls," Kate said. "I need to talk with my daughter and the people around her – make sure she's kept safe. She's pregnant and very vulnerable.

"I also need to call Jack's field foreman, Carlo Bernini. If Jack was concerned about a painting, he would have discussed it with Carlo. He lives in Rome and Jack was going to see him before he went to San Sebastiano."

"That's a good idea," Dair responded. "I can talk to the American authorities and let them know there's a serious threat to your daughter; emphasize this from a law enforcement perspective. I tried once yesterday to call Mr. Bernini, but I needed to get to the airport before you did to make sure you were safe, so I didn't pursue it.

"Unfortunately, Quinn and I have been a bit shorthanded. However, I've called in reinforcements and we can keep you safe now, unless you'd like to go home and be with your daughter."

"Not on your life, Mr. Munro," Kate said with a glare. "Liz has plenty of people to watch over her. Right now, Michael may be in serious trouble and I want him found. Then I want to be there when we find the people who murdered my husband.

"I have contacts and influence all over Europe; and a great deal of money at my disposal. I also suspect I can be of assistance to you if you need to get answers from museum personnel, or some of those Italian aristocrats you were talking about. So, let's not waste any more time, shall we?" she said firmly.

Dair shook his head. Somehow, he had known this lady was going to be a force to be reckoned with, and then some.

CHAPTER 9

The Cardinal

Afternoon in Rome
11 May 1975

The young priest quietly entered the elegant Vatican chamber and said, "Your Eminence, you have a visitor who does not have an appointment. He insisted I ask if you could see him, now."

Ignacio Cardinal Messina raised his eyes from the paper he was reading and surveyed the priest who had interrupted him. "Does this man have a name?" he asked.

"Yes, your Eminence," the young assistant almost stammered. "His name is Sergio Antonelli. He said you would know why he has come."

Cardinal Messina made a shooing motion with his hand and said, "Very well. Show him in. How many minutes do I have before the meeting with the finance committee starts?"

"It does not start for half an hour, Your Eminence. Would you like me to give you a warning five minutes before you need to leave?" the priest asked.

"Yes, that might help hurry my visitor on his way. Thank you, Paolo," he said and returned his gaze to the desk. This concealed the anger that was building inside him at the fool who would soon be standing before him.

Antonelli entered the Cardinal's chambers with quaking knees. He had handled the task he'd been given very badly. He did not know what this Prince of the Church would do. It would probably not be good.

"Your Eminence, thank you for seeing me on such short notice. I humbly beg your pardon for this intrusion," he began obsequiously.

The Cardinal raised his hand for silence. "I am very disappointed in the outcome of the task I set you, Sergio. I believe I asked you to proceed with great diplomacy and discretion. What possessed you to hire that fool who showed no such qualities?" he asked quietly.

"I know, Your Eminence, and I had planned to meet the plane myself when it was originally scheduled to arrive. However, I had a family emergency yesterday afternoon and was detained. I have known Luigi since his childhood and he has always been such a devoted son of the Church. He knew only that this woman was to be intercepted before she got into Rome so we could have a quiet conversation with her. Apparently, he thought it was more of a cloak and dagger operation.

"He's young. Unfortunately, his grandmother was the wrong person to be a conspirator in this endeavor. He left her with the perception that Mrs. Evans presented a danger to the

Church and must be hidden at all costs. He did not even know there was a gun in the house. When the police came to the door, she was prepared to defend the Church to her death," he related.

"All of this is most unfortunate," said Messina. "Of course, steps must be taken to assure there is no connection between the man or his grandmother and the Church hierarchy. The fact that Interpol was following Mrs. Evans predisposes me to think we are skating on very thin ice. We will have to use another avenue to discover how much the lady knows about the letter.

"For now, send Luigi to Avignon to work with our brothers there. Tell him we will have masses said for his grandmother's soul for the rest of the year. And you, forget everything that's happened in the past three days. Forget about Mrs. Evans. Have I made myself clear? You are to have no further part in our search for the truth."

Antonelli swallowed and got his voice under control. "Yes, Eminence, I will do as you wish. My only desire is to be of service to you and the Holy Father."

Cardinal Messina watched as he bowed himself out of the chamber. He sighed, realizing that this was not the end of the problem. All of this over a letter that might or might not exist from that idiot, Dr. Francesco Petacci. Had rumors of its existence been true? Something had started the rumor, or someone, and it was a tangle that someone else must unravel.

Had the death of Pius XI been unnatural; happening just hours before a meeting he'd called of all the bishops in Italy to denounce Hitler and the Nazi party? Had death been helped along by a syringe in the hands of a Vatican doctor? Had the act been admitted to in writing by that doctor? If so, who had the letter now?

This was a Jesuitical problem with many aspects, so maybe a Jesuit was the man to untangle it. He needed to see his old friend, Monsignor Giovanni Larosa, to pick his brain.

"Your Eminence," said Father Paolo, "It is time for you to leave for the meeting."

"Thank you, Paolo. Is my car out front?" he asked as he rose and placed his red hat on his head. Paolo indicated that all was ready and held the door.

Later that evening, following evening prayers, he sat by the fire in his study. The month of May could still have chilly evenings and he was getting old enough to enjoy this indulgence. He'd finished his work with the international finance committee and now he had the luxury of time to plan his next actions.

In a few minutes, Monsignor Larosa of the Vatican's Jesuit School, joined him for a glass of cognac. They had known and respected each other for 30 years. They had never, though, discussed the topic on his mind tonight.

"Gianni, I have a hypothetical problem I'd like to discuss with you and perhaps you can suggest a solution," he said, opening the discussion.

"Of course, Your Eminence, I always enjoy our hypothetical jousting. What's on your mind?" he said, shifting to get comfortable in the well-padded armchair.

"First, let's take a little trip back in time to the early 1930s when Achille Ratti, our beloved Pope Pius XI, was bishop in Austria. He'd been a scholar, earning three doctorates in his studies. He'd been head of the Vatican Library and, astonishingly, he was a fearless, almost reckless mountain climber.

"His time in Austria coincided with the rise to power of a young Adolf Hitler; and Ratti at first admired him. Hitler was fanatically anti-Communist, and so was Mussolini and much of Italy.

"Eventually, he would come to hate the gospel Hitler was preaching about the master race. He feared the anti-Semitic hyperbole was leading Germany and its allies toward a war with the rest of Europe. He did a lot of diplomatic work for Pope Benedict XV, and as a reward, he was named a Cardinal when he returned in August of 1921. But he never forgot what he'd seen and heard of Hitler."

"Yes," the Monsignor said, "I recall some of that, although I was very young and I think what I really remember is being told a lot of this when I arrived in Rome."

The Cardinal continued, "Yes, that's how I learned most of his history, too. He'd only worn his red hat for a year when his mentor, Benedict, died. He was attending his first gathering of cardinals to name a new Pope. He was a compromise candidate for the honor.

"Another cardinal had turned it down, and they were on the 14th ballot. But he won the white hat and carried on like he'd won on the first ballot. I understand he always ate alone, never in public, and even his brother and sister had to make appointments to see him. They also had to refer to him as Holy Father, never by his given name."

The Monsignor smiled and sipped his cognac. "In short, he literally believed he was chosen by God, not the Cardinals. That can be a dangerous path."

"Indeed," agreed Messina. "He made it his business to protest Adolf Hitler's every move for the next 10 years or so. He sent an encyclical to Germany to be read from the pulpit in every Catholic Church denouncing war, anti-Semitism, annexation of property, mass arrests, everything. All that did was enrage Hitler and he arrested thousands of priests, nuns, bishops, Catholic laymen; and he confiscated Church property."

"As I recall," the Monsignor said, "that didn't stop the Holy Father. I believe it was he who negotiated the Lateran Treaty that gave independence to the state of the Vatican. He and Mussolini carved up Italy, with the Vatican tending souls and Mussolini running the trains on time."

"All true," the Cardinal said. "That worked for a time, but eventually Hitler became a threat and Pius XI wouldn't keep silent. When Hitler made his one trip to Rome, Mussolini rolled out the red carpet. It's thought the visit cost Italy about $2 million in 1930s currency.

"In the meantime, Pius XI pointedly left town to visit Castel Gondolfo for a retreat. He also closed the Vatican Museum and left instructions no one was to visit in his absence. And, he told the Vatican newspaper not to write anything about Hitler and his visit. In short, he made sure the Vatican ignored the Führer in no uncertain terms."

Messina continued. "All this time, the College of Cardinals was shaking in its collective sandals. They feared reprisals from Hitler if the Pope spoke too harshly. Also, some of them agreed with Hitler and his anti-Semitic stance.

"Pius took no notice. In fact, he called them to come to Rome in February of 1939, for a personal meeting with him. He had asked one of your brethren, an American Jesuit named John LaFarge, to help him write an encyclical he planned to present at this meeting denouncing Hitler and his policies."

The Cardinal stopped long enough to tend the logs in the fireplace, then settled back down.

"His health had slowed him down. He had what everyone thought was a heart attack in 1936 when he was 78, and everyone thought because of his age, he would die soon.

"But he hung on for another year, and was busy setting up the meeting. Less than twelve hours before the Congress was to convene, he died. Cardinal Pacelli, who was the Vatican Secretary of State, had each of the 300 copies of the encyclical gathered up and destroyed. He then took care of getting the Pope buried and his effects removed from the Papal apartments."

The Monsignor continued the story. "As I recall, Pacelli was then named Pope Pius XII, and steered a very neutral path through the war. However, it was said he was quietly active in assisting hundreds of escaping Jews to leave Italy; all very under-the-radar."

Messina agreed and picked up the narrative. "So, did someone, fearing what Mussolini would do to the Church, take steps to make sure the Pope didn't live to present the encyclical? Or, was it all a case of the heart of an 80-year-old man, who drove himself unmercifully, finally wearing out?

"In which case, why would a Vatican doctor confess, in a letter, to poisoning the Pope? The fact that Dr. Francesco Petacci was a member of the Vatican Medical Services and was also the father of Mussolini's mistress, Clara Petacci, gave fuel to the whispers. Was it just a whisper that Eugène Cardinal Tisserant is said to have written in his diary? He apparently wrote that Pius XI was murdered."

Monsignor Larosa was silent for a while, then asked, "Do you know?"

"How could I know, my friend," Messina said, cocking an eyebrow. "This is all just a hypothetical conversation."

"Why are you sharing this with me? And why now?" the Monsignor inquired.

"Dr. Petacci died five years ago, without, to my knowledge, saying anything about 1939. Shortly after that, the whispers started again. If it could be true, that such a letter exists, I want to find it and destroy it before it harms the Church we serve," Messina admitted.

"Do you think it could really damage the Church after all this time. It happened so long ago, before WWII. Does anyone care anymore?" Larosa asked.

"We're talking about the Pope who became the first Pope of the Vatican State, as a result of a deal with Mussolini. He loved science and inventions. He founded Vatican Radio and gave regular sermons over it to reach out to those within sound of his voice. He appeared in newsreels that were shown around the world and his face spread far beyond the borders of Italy, often for the first time in history.

"The Papacy is held in even higher esteem now than it was in the 1930s when it served 350 million souls. The men who have become popes since Pius XII have been men of unimpeachable honesty and character. They have become instruments of peaceful progress.

"To admit that someone murdered one of their predecessors to change a political course is so reprehensible that I think it would take decades to recover from the scandal," Messina said.

"And what do you want from me," the Monsignor asked. "You want something, or we wouldn't be having this discussion – hypothetical as it might be."

Messina said, "I want you to recommend someone to find out for me. Someone in whom you have complete faith, who is intelligent and competent; without more bloodshed. I have four names that might be helpful, two of whom are Americans who are often in Europe.

"They are Kate and Michael Evans, a mother and son, who have a great deal of wealth and many friends in Italy. Then an SS Colonel Werner Lang, who is undoubtedly using another name now, and Carlo Bernini, an archeologist who lives in Rome. I can give the individual you choose more information on them, but I think we have the best chance of finding an answer from one of them."

He paused for a moment before finally confiding the last piece of information.

"An informant came to me some time ago saying that if there was a letter, it was possibly the one that was with a cargo of paintings stored in the crypt of the San Sebastiano Martire church during the war.

"This man said that when Jack Evans, an American, was in San Sebastiano after WWII, there was a chance he found the letter and the paintings. He died five years ago in an accident near the town. I was told it was because of a letter that he was going back there," the Cardinal concluded.

"Is this Kate Evans the one who is in the papers tonight as having been kidnapped, resulting in the death of an old woman who attacked an Italian police officer?" Larosa said with more than a touch of asperity. "And who was this informant?"

"Yes," the Cardinal admitted with a sigh. "It's the same Mrs. John Evans and it was badly handled. I rarely make a mistake as egregious as this one. As to the informant, it was a man who deals in secrets.

"Whether or not he was telling the truth, I don't know. That's why I need the help of an intelligent man who can sift through the complexities of this situation and give me an answer. If he discovers the letter exists, I want it found. Can you recommend someone?

The Monsignor sat silently for two or three minutes. Finally, he stirred and said, "I think I have someone who might help you. I'll call him in and see what he says. He's very good, but once he starts, he will insist on finding an answer. You must be prepared for whatever it is."

The Cardinal said, "Thank you, my friend. I will leave this in your more than capable hands."

CHAPTER 10

The Colonel

Hotel Cavaliere
11 May 1975

Standing silently in the shadows that surrounded the Piazza Margutta, former SS Colonel Werner Lang had watched young Evans depart without being seen last night. Now comfortably situated in his hotel room with a snifter of cognac, he had time to reflect on that entire episode.

The boy had done a good job of moving silently in and out of the old man's apartment. Of course, he couldn't know that Lang had preceded him by a couple of hours and had patiently waited for anyone else who might show up.

He'd also watched the boy's mother come down the concourse at the airport and get into that rather ill-fated private car. As he stood by the newsvendor's stand wearing sunglasses, he'd also watched the two Interpol agents who had followed her. At that point, he'd decided there was no point in adding to the parade.

His driver dropped him at the Hotel Cavalieri, where he was also a registered guest. He was not, however, registered as Werner Lang. He'd gone through several sobriquets since he'd been Lang. Now, he was a Swiss banker named Paul Bauer. He'd changed his name so many times in the past 30 years that he liked to keep them short, easier to remember.

Since his return to Europe from South America, he had been involved in dozens of profitable activities. He'd also provided work for a vast network of street people who could find out anything he wanted to know in a short period of time. He'd find Kate Evans, and Michael, whenever he was ready.

He knew Michael had recently been in Viet Nam. The information was passed on by an informer who'd been keeping an eye on his old colleague, Lt. Hesse. Hesse had also changed his name again and moved on to greener pastures; but Lang liked to keep an eye on him. Hesse knew about the paintings they had stashed in the old church. What he had never known was what the metal box contained.

Lang had only found that out when he'd witnessed the Führer venting his spleen at Mussolini's ineffectual attempt to stay in power. That's when he'd let it slip about the box containing something that Il Duce could use to his advantage against the Vatican. When he'd had the chance, he'd taken the letter before leaving the box in the crypt.

His had been an interesting relationship with Hitler. They had first met through an American, of all things. Although Ernst Hanfstaengl, nicknamed 'Putzi', would have argued that he was more German than American.

Nonetheless, his mother was an American who married the son of a wealthy German publisher.

Putzi had spent time in both Germany and America before attending Harvard in the early 1900s. The gifted pianist even wrote fight songs for the Harvard football team. After graduation, he'd stayed in New York and taken over his father's fine arts publications. He spent time at the Harvard Club, where he met both Franklin and Theodore Roosevelt, and made friends with everyone from Randolph Hearst to Charlie Chaplin.

He had returned to Bavaria in the 1920s and hired a promising young man named Werner Lang to act as his secretary. Lang was fascinated by everything American. He was also interested in Putzi's world of arts, museums and wealth. That lifestyle dazzled young Lang.

In 1929, they went to hear a failed young painter, Adolph Hitler, talk about what was wrong with Germany. Putzi went as a favor to an old friend stationed at the American embassy in Berlin. The officer wanted to know what Putzi thought of the guy who was stirring things up in the Munich beer halls.

Putzi was so enthralled, he became a disciple. He'd taken young Lang along with him on the climb up the political ladder. When the infamous Beer Hall Putsch occurred in 1923, Lang helped an injured Hitler hide in Putzi's home in Munich. Hitler had never forgotten his help. Putzi, of course, had run to Austria.

In 1931, as Hitler became more politically acceptable, they both joined the Nazi Party. Lang became a member of the inner circle around Hitler. They talked about art as well as politics. Hitler felt he'd been robbed of a great career as a painter by established artists who twice refused him entrance to the Vienna Academy of Fine Arts. He loved the great Masters, especially those of the German and Flemish schools, and detested the new ranks of Impressionist painters.

Putzi was as fluent in English as he was in German, and had many connections in both England and the United States. It was natural decision to make him the head of the Foreign Press Bureau in Berlin. That put him in control of the news copy being sent out of Germany in the 1930s. However, it also was the end of his acceptance in the Allied world when word of his relationship with Hitler spread.

Lang's influence with Hitler also grew rapidly. He joined the German Army and became an officer in the SS, always assigned to Hitler's staff. By 1939, Putzi was out of favor and out of office. He moved his family to Switzerland to sit out the war. His donations to Harvard's fundraisers were returned.

Hitler had overreached his abilities by 1944 when he sent Lang to Italy to oversee the bribe payment. He was using narcotics that blocked his ability to reason, but was aware there were plots among the German officers to assassinate him.

By 1945, Lang had his plans firmly in place. He had enough money in accounts in neutral Switzerland – neutral, but happy to take money from any German bank or officer – to support him in retirement.

Two weeks before Hitler committed suicide, Lang slipped across the French border with paperwork that would stand up to close Allied scrutiny. He became Adolphus De Vries, a Dutch art dealer who had been in hiding, fearing for his life. Once the identity was affirmed, he took a little trip to Rio de Janeiro to let things cool for a decade.

Then he was back in Paris, reconnecting with the Bony-LaFont gang. They had been known as the French Gestapo. If some wealthy collector, Jewish or otherwise, came on their radar, they stripped the family of everything.

The days of Nazi occupation in Paris became a free-for-all for every sewer rat in the city. French families that had lived like kings were rounded up or fled before they could be captured; leaving everything behind. Silver, gold, gems, paintings, sculpture, tapestries, antique furniture, clocks, and china in great profusion fell to the gangs and their moving vans.

The Germans would offer bills of sale for some of the rarest items, particularly the paintings, so that they could be shipped to Switzerland where art sales were booming. Many of the priceless pieces were sold, then sold again by Sotheby's, Christies, and smaller galleries.

Private collectors had entrée to these cut-rate auctions and filled their homes. After the war, there would be little chance of finding the original owners or their heirs having any claim to their family's treasures.

People who worked with the Nazi regime made money and wanted to spend it on something. Many turned to the lucrative art market. Hitler didn't want Impressionist paintings, but the French did – at least the art that avoided the mass bonfires.

They stimulated a huge market in works by Cezanne, Degas, Monet, Renoir and Corot because they believed they would be worth more after the war; no matter who won.

Lang and his confederates had stored their treasure troves in Swiss bank vaults for several years. Once he was back in town, they became adept at turning these 'abandoned goods' into fortunes.

His success in the black market provided the launching pad for his career as an intermediary for men and countries seeking bigger and better armament. Whether it was rifles, bombs or planes, he could promote a sale. If someone needed an assassin, he could even provide that. In a pinch, he could come up with an entire mercenary army. Death was a booming business all over the planet!

He had been amazed at the men who had killed the old archeologist. They just sat out front, stupidly expecting one of the Evans family to come marching through the front door. Their boss would not have been happy had he known. Would he be showing up soon?

What could he expect from cheap hoodlums? Not like the first-class players the Vatican could marshal, always excepting the dunce who'd kidnapped Kate Evans. They would do better next time, he was sure.

He'd been busy spreading a great deal of disinformation about the Evans family and their interests in San Sebastiano; at least enough to keep the red hats on Vatican Hill off balance. Poor Cardinal Messina.

Yes, the game was going to be interesting, he thought as he refilled his cognac. He felt rather smug about knowing all the players in what appeared to be an interesting game of cat and mouse.

It looked like it was going to be a competition among the gang who had stolen the paintings from the crypt; the Evans-Interpol team; and the Vatican and their minions – all looking for answers to the same question. Who had the contents of the San Sebastiano crypt?

He might decide to weigh in on one side or the other. Or, since age was beginning to catch up with him a bit, he might just sit on the sidelines and see what happened; like a referee. He found that idea made him smile – just a little.

CHAPTER 11

The Contessa

Parioli Palazzos
11 May 1975

Kate Evans stood at the Interpol room's single window, trying to see a landmark that would tell her where she was. She whirled as the door opened and Dair Munro walked in waving a piece of paper.

"Your son is in Rome. He called the hotel and left a message. It's a bit strange," he said.

"He's often somewhat obscure in his messages. He used to invent codes to use with Liz, then left the rest of us trying to decipher them. What did he say?" she asked.

"He told them to tell you that he was okay, and then he signed off with *tata for now*," he said. "Does that give us a clue as to his whereabouts?"

Kate could see his skin furrow between his eyes as he tried to divine what kind of Army Ranger would say *tata*. It slightly amused Kate, but she was also momentarily at a loss. Michael wasn't really into the English habit of saying *tata* on departure, but she could be wrong.

After all, he'd spent all that time in England studying and touring. She knew he loved the English afternoon tea habit – especially anything chocolate. She'd often seen both Liz and Michael with their noses pressed against a pastry cafe's window, trying to decide if this place had the right kind of cake for tea break. But there was no reason he'd used that phrase in Rome, so what did he mean?

Suddenly, the penny dropped.

"Oh, I know what he meant, and it's brilliant. No one hearing or seeing that message would have any idea," she exclaimed with a smile.

"Uh-huh, and I would be one of them. What's with the *tata*?" Dair asked.

"Oh, sorry. Just a mother being proud of her tricky little boy. And the secret lies in the little boy part. When he and Liz were children and we lived in Rome, they had a sort of nanny, which in Italian is..." she got no further.

"Yes! *Tata* is a nickname for an Italian nanny. So presumably, when he couldn't find you, he headed for a safe haven and left clear directions, at least clear for you," he finished for her.

"Exactly. I think Gina and her family have lived in the same block for generations. I'm sure they must still be here. Now I have to see if I have her address with me or whether I'll have to call Liz to have her look for it on my Christmas card list," she said, rummaging through the purse that had finally been returned to her.

"Rats," she said, tossing down her bag. "I cleaned out my purse to lighten the load before I got on the plane. One of the things I left behind was my address book. Well, looks like I'll have to bother Liz. I hate to do that. It's only 3 a.m. in New Haven. She's not been sleeping well now that she's getting closer to delivery."

"Well, normally, I'd have you give me Gina's last name and I'd get Interpol busy finding her. But this isn't normally. Quinn and I believe we have a high-level leak in the organization, someone who is getting a piece of the action from all the millions changing hands," Dair said. "I'm not sure I trust even the Interpol lines right now."

Quinn O'Malley had been standing near the door and said, "What about your godmother, Contessa d'Este? She'd be thrilled to help you. You know she's got contacts all over the city and in circles even Interpol can't reach. She's also got phone lines that are clear. I think Giuseppe makes sure of that."

Dair stopped and thought for a minute.

"There are a number of upsides to that," he said. "Her phones certainly wouldn't be compromised; she loves secrets; and she gets up with the birds. There's only one downside," he said.

"Well, what's that," Kate asked impatiently.

"She is the biggest gossip I know," he admitted. "We're going to have to work around this without her knowing who you are."

Quinn grinned, then said, "We'll just have to talk Giuseppe into making it happen."

"Giuseppe?" Kate queried.

"Yes, he's the Contessa's right-hand man. You have to get through him to reach Bridget. Anything she wants done, he does it, or gets the right person to do it. And when it comes to secrets, he's like the tomb. I'm not sure I've ever heard him say much more than 'Si, La Contessa.' Then it miraculously gets done," Dair said.

"Can we just show up, with no warning, so early in the morning?" Kate asked. "If we don't want to let anyone know where we're going, I don't see how we can warn her."

"That's no problem," Dair said breezily. "She adores Quinn, here, since she was also born in Ireland. He can enchant her with a few of his stories while you and I work with Giuseppe. But we need to move as soon as you are ready," he added.

"I've washed my face; brushed my teeth; and combed my hair; thanks to the toothbrush and comb you provided. I regret to say that I have no way to change clothes. I look forward to being reunited with my luggage at some point," Kate retorted. "I'm as ready as I'll ever be. I want to see Michael. There is so much I don't understand and I think he may have more pieces to this puzzle."

"Do you have some way to cover your distinctive hair?" Dair asked. "Also, put on these sunglasses and maybe turn your jacket inside out. I don't want to make recognizing you any easier than necessary."

"I can't turn the jacket. The seams would show. I was trying to travel light on this trip, not realizing I was going to need everything I owned," she said with some exasperation.

"What about that sweater of yours and your rain hat?" Quinn said to Dair. "They are in the back of the car. The sweater's going to be big, but she's pretty tall, so it might pass inspection."

"OK, go get them and we'll get on the road," Dair said.

A few minutes later, they were wending through the crowded streets of central Rome on the way to the northern suburb of Parioli, home to the chic, elegant and wealthy.

The Contessa lived in a palazzo in an area of other oversized estates. An eight-foot wrought iron fence, interwoven with stands of blooming shrubs, protected the approach to the house. The ornate gates swung open after Quinn requested entrance through the call box.

After winding through more trees, the building appeared suddenly with an air of gracefully aging grandeur. Silvered sprays of water danced from three large fountains as the car made a final turn into the horseshoe drive, stopping before the house.

The door was already opening when they approached the stairs. An imposing man of uncertain age, but beautifully barbered silver hair, waited for them.

"Giuseppe, so good to see you again," Dair greeted him. "I hope we're not too early to visit with the Contessa.

"I'm sure the Contessa will be delighted to see you, as always, Mr. Munro," Giuseppe said with a welcoming gesture to enter. "And you, Mr. O'Malley." Then, as they entered, he looked pointedly at Kate – hatted, sunglassed and draped in a sweater three sizes too large.

"Giuseppe, this is a guest of mine, Kate Kelly. She's going to need some help from you and the Contessa," Dair explained, hearing quick footsteps approaching.

Kate didn't know who or what she expected to meet, but it was not the slim, elegant sprite with a head of snow-white hair who entered the room to hug first, Dair, and then Quinn. Clad in a cloud of pink chiffon dressing gown, she turned lively blue eyes on Kate and lifted an eyebrow to Dair.

"And who do we have here, Alisdair," she inquired, "someone whose been ensnared in one of your ghastly Interpol plots."

The Contessa graciously gestured for them all to sit in a drawing room roughly the size of a bowling alley. As they settled on stunning antique sofas, Kate wondered what excuse he was going to use for showing up at such an unorthodox hour. She quickly shed the borrowed hat and sunglasses.

"Now, Bridget," Dair said, "not everyone I know has to be connected with work. This is Kate Kelly, an American who is touring some of the gardens of Italy. We have mutual friends in England who suggested I give her an introduction to you.

"Your gardens are the toast of Rome and I told her I was sure you'd be happy to let her peek. Unfortunately, we need to leave town quite soon, and knowing you're an early riser, I hoped we could impose on you this morning."

A little lame, but Munro was doing the best he could. However, Kate had seen the intelligence in those blue eyes before the Contessa lowered her lashes and gave a gracious smile.

"Of course, I'm delighted to share my flowers. Do you have special favorites you'd like to see, Miss Kelly?" she asked.

Kate, who had outstanding flower beds circling her New Haven home, owned that she would be enchanted to see anything the Contessa felt like sharing.

"Well, then we'll step outside and let the gentlemen have some coffee. Giuseppe, you'll see to it?" she questioned. At his nod, she turned toward French doors leading to the courtyard. Then she stopped and turned.

"Oh, Alisdair dear, I just started a letter to you about Angus. I was so sorry to hear of his passing, but at least he didn't linger. We both know how much he'd have hated being an invalid.

"This has got to be very difficult for you. I'd like to speak with you further about your plans when you have time. His passing of the clan's torch to you must mean some drastic changes for the future."

With that parting shot, she led Kate toward a flower-bedecked gateway at the rear of the house. As they walked, Kate sought some commonplace topic for conversation.

"How is it that an Irish-Italian Contessa is the godmother of a Scottish Interpol agent," she inquired lightly.

"Oh my, that's a long but interesting story. I can shorten it, however," the Contessa said. "My mother was the sister of Angus Munro's father, who was also the Laird of Munro;

so, Angus and I were first cousins. She married a rascally Irish earl who lived in Dublin. I was their only child and when Angus' nephew, Alisdair, was born, I was asked to be his godmother.

"My husband, Antonio, was the second son of Count Lorenzo d'Este. During WWII, he left Italy and went to train in England to fight Mussolini. His family stayed here; I think mostly to guard the family's properties. He met Angus and started training with his band of special forces.

"At the same time, I left neutral Ireland and went to do my bit in Scotland. I had been driving since I was 16 and could handle the big supply trucks on those twisting Scottish roads. I delivered things to Angus' compound," she said.

She made a show of pointing out some lush mauve azaleas as they passed, then continued.

"I met Antonio, fell madly in love with his curly black hair and his gorgeous smile. He seemed to feel the same way about me, and we eloped. I have no idea what his family thought, but they couldn't have been pleased. An Irish woman!

"However, that will always remain unknown because when the Nazis occupied Italy in 1944, they rounded up a good share of the nobility who hadn't already fled and sent them to camps," she said, stopping for a few moments.

"They were already having trouble feeding their troops, so they didn't waste a lot of food on prisoners, even important ones. By then, Mussolini, whom I think my father-in-law believed would protect them, had no influence. In any case, they died. First the count, then his wife, and finally Antonio's older brother and sister.

"When he came back after the war, there was no one left. We spent the next five years trying to regain his property and take care of his people. Fortunately, most of the assets had been banked in Switzerland, so we weren't exactly penniless," she said with a small laugh.

"However, the house had been ransacked. The priceless art, carpets, tapestries – all gone. The staff had gone into hiding, taking a few of the most precious artifacts, but they had suffered.

"That broke Antonio's heart. My gay, laughing boy disappeared to be replaced by one who only rarely smiled. Mussolini and Hitler laid a scar across Europe that hasn't healed yet."

Guiding Kate through the garden, she ended up in a small gazebo overlooking yet another pond and fountain.

Gesturing toward a seat, she said, "And now, Mrs. Evans, I think it's time to, as they say, lay our cards on the table. Of course, I recognize you. Your face has graced far too many fashion magazines for me not to have. We also share several friends who love to gossip about your lively family when they get the chance. I, of course, never gossip. I can, however, see you are in great distress and I read about your experience at the airport.

"When I add in the presence of my darling cousin and Mr. O'Malley, I would have to be a great deal less intelligent than I am to believe the taradiddle Alisdair is trying to sell me. Whatever your reason for being here, looking like a badly-dressed gypsy, it isn't my gardens. Why don't you tell me what's wrong and I'll lend you all the assistance I can – including my dear Giuseppe."

Kate paused a beat, then said, "Well, Contessa, I'm not completely sure myself what's going on. Mr. Munro and I may have different purposes. He and Mr. O'Malley are involved with trying to stop illicit trade in black market art works. Those works include pieces believed destroyed in WWII. Now, however, they think those are being sold by a central, organized gang that's leaving a trail of dead bodies behind them.

"This is where I come in. My purpose is more personal. Mr. Munro believes my husband was murdered by this same gang because he had been asked by the niece of one of the murder victims to come to Italy," Kate said.

"I want to find the truth and help put a stop to the slaughter before it can reach my children and grandchildren. Yes, I was kidnapped when I arrived in Rome yesterday. That's how I met Mr. Munro. He and Mr. O'Malley rescued me before whomever did it could injure me further. I'll do anything I can to stop this. I have powerful friends who can put pressure on people and events, but I need to find a place to start," she stopped to take a breath.

"My son is currently in hiding here in Rome and while we know with whom he's staying, we don't have an address. Mr. Munro believes someone at Interpol may have been corrupted by this illegal conspiracy. He says there's too much money involved for this gang not to have influence in high places. So, he's planning to use your phone lines to contact a few people he trusts. He's also going to speak with Giuseppe about any contacts he might have across the city who might help find Michael."

"And if that's not enough," she added dolefully, "I haven't been able to change my clothes in two days because my luggage is traveling around Rome without me. So, I do apologize for showing up at your door looking like, what did you call it, a 'badly dressed gypsy' at a ridiculously early hour."

The Contessa had listened thoughtfully as Kate spelled out her problems. She tapped a well-manicured finger on the arm of her chair and sat silently as she digested the news.

"I'm sure Alisdair told you I have a reputation as a terrible gossip and, perhaps, even a bit of a feather brain, which is partly true. What he doesn't know, since he spent so much time roaming the world with Angus, is that my reputation is carefully cultivated. I have Giuseppe to thank for that," she said.

"I may gossip, but I never give away anything unless I get something in return. I have an idea that you might start your inquiries with my friend Principessa Maria Louisa d'Sforza.

"She told me some disquieting news about a mutual acquaintance. It seems this person has an unusual art collection, some of which is seen by only a few discriminating people with similar tastes. If it's part of what you're looking for, that person might be able to tell you where and from whom the art came."

Kate rose and said, "Let's get Mr. Munro and let him hear all this first-hand. It will save time, and we can watch his face as he realizes how badly he's underestimated you."

As they walked hurriedly back to the villa, Kate did realize the extensive gardens had been designed by a master. He or she had created a faux painting using a palette of pinks, segueing into purple, then blue, and yellows. The designer had also added texture and proportion to make the vista one of harmony and beauty. She'd like to return to spend time in this peaceful setting someday.

Back in the villa, they found Munro and O'Malley in deep conversation with Giuseppe.

"Mr. Munro," Kate began before he could speak, "the Contessa has something very important to tell you."

Dair cast a questioning eye at the pair. Evidently, that walk in the garden had produced more than admiration for the flowers.

"What is it?" he asked.

"Well, to start with," Kate said, "your very sharp-eyed godmother was onto you before you opened your mouth. She recognized me as Kate Evans, charming sweater and all. And that's not all she knows. She may trade in gossip – or exchange information as she would prefer to say – but nothing gets past her. I'll let her tell you."

"Alisdair, darling, Kate tells me you're looking for artworks that have been surfacing on the black market.

Paintings that were stolen during WWII and listed as destroyed.

"I have heard rumblings in some quarters related to this, and I've kept my ears open, especially since all the art in this villa was stolen and has never been returned," she said.

She gestured toward the silver-haired man as she continued.

"Giuseppe was a young retainer to Antonio's family when the war started. He saw all the terrible things that happened to the city and the family. After the family was taken, he joined the Resistance and helped blow up train tracks and steal food for the starving population.

"Needless to say, he has built up a network of friends over the years that extends across the city. Very little happens of importance that he does not know about. I'm guessing that's what you are attempting to access today in your conversation with him," she said, raising another eyebrow.

"Yes, you are right, Bridget. And I humbly apologize for so grievously underestimating your influence in the goings-on of the city," he said, with a slight bow. "I shall never again call your information-gathering 'gossip'."

"Apology accepted, my dear," the Contessa said. "Now, here is what I told Kate. My friend, the Principessa Maria d'Sforza, and I were discussing a mutual acquaintance last week. His name is Umberto Malaggi. He made a great deal of money during the war, in ways we're pretty sure were not legitimate. But he's never been charged in regard to war crimes, black market activities, or anything.

"He has continued to make large piles of money, if his expenditures are any guide as to his resources. Given that he may not be the most scrupulous of characters, I was surprised when Maria said he'd recently given a party for a small group of prominent art collectors."

She shrugged and continued.

"The halls of his villa are covered with artworks, most of moderate to so-so execution. He has a few favored artists that he patronizes and some of their work may be valuable in the future, but not today. He has two major works that even I would like to own, and he undoubtedly spent a great deal of money on those. One is a Cezanne and the other is a Monet."

"It is said, in certain circles, that he has other masterpieces in his possession that do not hang on the walls upstairs," the Contessa continued. "I've heard whispers that he has a subterranean gallery with other art work. No one I know has ever said what kind it is, but I get the feeling it's not erotic or anything equally repelling.

"I think it might be fruitful for you, if you're searching for an organization that is flogging stolen masterpieces, to talk with Umberto. He might be able to give you the name of his supplier, especially if some pressure could be brought to bear about the consequences of his business dealings."

Dair felt like laughing. That his darling Irish cousin had held the answer to his search in the palm of her small hand was truly unbelievable. It was a humbling lesson in not judging books by their covers.

"Bridget, I am awestruck," he said. "When the trail of this gang led to Rome, I should have been on your doorstep immediately. Between you and Giuseppe, you must know every secret in the Seven Hills. We will, indeed, be interviewing Signore Malaggi very soon. Now, if you can unearth the address for Gina Ghilberti, our cups will be full."

"Mrs. Evans, if I may ask," said Giuseppe, "did you ever visit Signorina Ghiberti at her home when she was your nanny?"

Kate had to think for a moment.

"Yes, I seem to remember that we did need to pick her up one time. She took a lot of luggage with her when we went to Herculaneum for the summer. Let me see if I can orient myself enough to remember what neighborhood she was in. It was 20 years ago," she said.

"I'm sorry to be so sluggish this morning. I don't think the effects of the knockout drug I was given have completely worn off yet. But I know Gina lived in the Trastevere, not too far from the Santa Cecilia Church. I think it was on Via Anica," she said, finally pulling the information from her foggy brain.

"That's very helpful, Madam," Giuseppe said with a bow and hurriedly left the room.

"Giuseppe has a friend in almost every neighborhood," the Contessa said soothingly. "I'm sure if the family is still there, we'll be able to give you her address very soon."

Kate appreciated the Contessa's moral support and finally realized she was hungry. She hadn't had a bite to eat since she'd left the plane. Because she'd been drugged, her sleep wasn't natural or restful. She was really flagging. She searched her mind for a polite way to ask for food.

As if he had read her mind, Dair said, "Bridget, if it wouldn't be too much trouble, I'd kill for a cup of coffee and I suspect Mrs. Evans needs something as well. It's been a while since her last meal."

"I should have known you didn't take the time to feed her before you showed up," the Contessa said, rising to her feet. She pulled a cord hanging next to a rococo-style mantle. A young man appeared as if by magic in answer to the summons.

"Nicolo, would you ask Cook to prepare breakfast for us now. There will be four of us. And, set the small table in the conservatory. Thank you," she said.

Dismissed, the servant hurried to carry out her wishes. Soon, they were being ushered through a warren of exquisite rooms to a table basking in the warm sun shining through the glass roof. Kate was gratified to see both tea and coffee sitting ready for pouring as she settled in her chair.

In ten minutes, a sumptuous breakfast, featuring an egg casserole, fresh croissants, fruit juices and breakfast meats, was on the table, served family style. As Kate took her first sip of hot tea, she felt a surge of hope that things were going to turn out all right for her family and for Dair Munro.

While the guests ate breakfast with the Contessa, Giuseppe was busy in his office on the telephone. The Contessa had been right about his having friends everywhere, but even she didn't know the extent of his contacts. As he dialed one number after another, his thoughts strayed to the other two who'd been such a vital part of establishing this information network.

It had started when the Nazis took Rome. He had been unceremoniously thrown out of the villa after the arrest of the d'Este family. The other retainers had been older and soon found sanctuary with family members. He had been just 16 years old and had come from a suburb of Rome. His parents were dead and his older brother had been sucked up by the Italian army.

Alone on the streets of Rome with the enemy everywhere, he'd gravitated to one the schools run by the Catholic nuns. There he'd helped to keep them fed, as well as himself. He'd made friends with two other teenaged boys who were also waifs on the street. The three had become fast friends with a relationship that was just as strong today as it was 35 years ago.

He'd been known as Pepe in those days, a name given him by Carlo and Orso. Carlo had a large family in Rome, but most of the men had been conscripted by the army while the women spent their days trying to scrounge food for their children.

Orso was like Pepe. His family had been killed in the bombing early in 1944. He seemed to have a home with some monks, but even their food resources were strained. He was a big kid with a serious demeanor; but he excelled at coming up with elaborate plans to outwit first the Nazis and later the Allied troops.

The complex plans he developed still made Giuseppe shake his head. In the end, the trio managed to keep a group of nearly 400 women, children and nuns, along with the Jews hidden by the nuns, fed on a daily basis. It took cunning and planning on an impressive scale.

Carlo was the muscle. He rounded up a group of street urchins who were up for any tricks they could play on the Germans. They became well-known faces around two or three of the Nazi commissary units. The Germans never realized that the loads of potatoes, cabbages and loaves of bread they sent out were routinely pilfered by the dirty-faced kids.

Pepe was in charge of distribution. He had another group of kids and women who were able to secret the pilfered goods in their shawls, book bags, and baby buggies. Their pitiful appearance usually kept them from being stopped and searched by the German patrols.

Orso was the brains behind the plans and he spent his days roaming the city, looking at the German distribution centers and transportation routes. He could see that a loaded truck left untended for a few minutes by distracted drivers could be half emptied by the hungry Romans. No one was the wiser because they never took everything. They'd rearrange the cargo to hide the holes.

Once the Allies entered Rome, pickings got even better. The flow of food coming from transport ships seemed endless. Toward the end of the war, the American kitchen crews even colluded with the boys when they found out how many people they were feeding. The quality of their diets increased drastically from a few vegetables to make weak stews to lots of vegetables with pieces of meat.

By then, the danger and intrigue were over, as was the need for their skills. Carlo's family members began to return to Rome.

Pepe's d'Este family came back to open the villa and rehire all the staff that had survived the occupation. He became a valuable employee to the estate. When the Count died, the Contessa had turned to him for assistance and he had cared for her ever since.

Orso had disappeared for a few years, and both Pepe and Carlo had searched for him. Finally, he was discovered working for another organization, using the skills and guile he had developed on the streets of Rome.

All three of them still shared the same network of informers and observers they'd developed long ago. What Carlo knew, Pepe and Orso also knew.

Now, Giuseppe was going to tap into that network to help Kate Evans and her family. Little did she know that through Carlo, Giuseppe had long known about the activities of the Evans family. He was going to find Michael.

Carlo would never forgive him if anything happened to the young man who called him uncle. He was also going to find out why he had lost contact with Carlo. Orso was waiting in the wings to assist. Time for them to rally the troops again.

CHAPTER 12

Injured

Trastevere Neighborhood
11 May 1975

Unfortunately for Kate's hope that all would be well with her family, it was not destined to be. Umberto Malaggi would be instrumental in that. He was sitting in the office of the lavish palazzo he owned when the private phone on his inlaid-cherry desk rang. He looked at it with a frown.

As he answered it, a voice he dreaded said, "Call the second name on your list. I want his grandsons to go to apartment 4B at 73 Via Anica. There are two people in the apartment. I want them both dead. One of them was a US Army Ranger, so tell them they need to be careful. He's dangerous.

"And tell them if they botch this job as badly as the last one, I will be very unhappy. No mistakes. And they'll have to hurry because men from Interpol will be showing up there in less than an hour." With that, the connection was broken.

Malaggi had paled during this brief call. He wasn't used to being involved in the more violent activities of his associate. But he quickly opened the center drawer of the desk and pulled out a short list of phone numbers. He dialed the number and gave the man who answered the directive from Milo Constantine.

As breakfast ended at the Villa d'Este, Giuseppe entered the room.

"Mrs. Evans, I have a friend who lives near the Basilica of Saint Cecilia. He is going to check with some shopkeepers in the neighborhood. If Signorina Ghilberti still lives there, they will know where. And, it will not cause any comment, not like it would if outsiders came looking for her family. Word of his search should not spread to unfriendly ears," he concluded.

"Oh, thank you," she responded. "I'm extremely grateful."

After his report, the Contessa turned to Kate and said, "My dear, you must be very tired after the events of the past 24 hours. Would you like to lie down for a while until we have news? I have a bedroom that is all yours for as long as you like. As a matter of fact, it has a lovely bath attached. You can refresh yourself and I'm going to find you something to wear until you can be reunited with your luggage."

Kate turned to her, "Thank you Contessa, I would love a bath."

When Kate left the luxurious bathroom after 20 minutes in the tub, she found clean undergarments, a silk blouse and a warm paisley shawl arrayed on the bed. An attempt at pressing her sadly-abused camel trousers had also been made, so she felt as prepared to meet the new day as possible.

Unfortunately, there was no way she was going to fit into many of the elfin Contessa's clothes. Her arms and legs were definitely too long. She was thankful for the new shawl.

A knock on the door brought the Contessa bustling into the room to ask if she'd now like a brief nap.

"Thank you so much for your hospitality, but I'm afraid I'm not going to get any rest until I see my son and talk with him. If you don't mind, I'd love to sit out in the garden while Giuseppe works his magic," she said.

Thirty minutes later, Dair walked outside to find Kate sitting in a chair, her face turned to the sun and her eyes closed.

"Mrs. Evans, we have an answer. We know where Signorina Ghilberti lives and we have her telephone number. It's up to you whether we call first and warn the Ghilbertis or just go over and see if Michael is there, but the choice is yours."

"I think it's best if I call ahead. Michael will be expecting me to get in touch. If you believe these lines are not compromised, I want to give him some warning. He doesn't know I have Interpol in tow," Kate said. "And Mr. Munro, after all that we've gone through in the past 48 hours, I think you should call me Kate."

"I think you're right, about both things. You can call Michael to let him know company is coming and I'll call you

Kate if you call me Dair, or Alisdair, or anything but Mr. Munro," Dair said.

Kate sat in the library of the Contessa's home and dialed the number Giuseppe had handed her. She listened to the line ring, and had a quick intake of breath when it was answered.

"Pronto," a woman's voice answered.

After all these years, Kate couldn't be sure it was Gina, but she hoped it was.

"Gina, so glad to hear your voice; it's your Tia Caterina," she said in her best Italian. "I'm checking to see if the package we sent you has arrived safely."

"Si, just a moment," Kate could hear murmuring in the background and then a voice she recognized came on the line.

"Mom, it's great to hear your voice," Michael said. "Where are you?"

"I'm here in Rome, in the Parioli neighborhood. I need to see you as soon as possible. Can I come to you at Gina's?"

"Yes," Michael answered. "I have a lot to tell you, as well. How long will it take for you to get here?"

"I have a car and I'll be bringing a couple of people with me. They are agents from Interpol. I'll see you soon, darling, and we'll pool our resources. Love you," she said.

"Love you, too, Mom," Michael answered. "You can't get here too quickly as far as I'm concerned. Ciao."

As she hung up, Kate felt a slight pang. She'd had him briefly, and now he was out of reach again. She chided herself for being foolish. She'd found him; in a few minutes she'd have a chance to hug him, as well. Time to move and stop being silly.

As she exited the library, she saw that Dair and Quinn were waiting for her.

"Everything all right?" Dair asked.

"Yes, he's there and waiting for us. You have the address?" she asked.

"Right here, and the Contessa is loaning us the villa's runabout. It's a dusty black Fiat and there are hundreds of them in Rome. If anyone did trail us here, they won't be expecting the car switch. You can lie down in the back seat until we are a few blocks away," he said. "Let's go."

It was short work to load her into the car and head out the gates. Quinn was driving and he circled the neighborhood for a few minutes looking for anyone following them, then headed for the Trastevere.

It was a medieval neighborhood of narrow alleys that had once been home to the slaves of Rome. The streets were too narrow for large vehicles and parking was a nightmare. It was a poor man's home for centuries, but artists, bohemians, and tourists had found it in the 1970s.

Quinn followed the convoluted directions Giuseppe had given them, pulling up behind a respectable looking apartment building. As they entered the front door, a scream rang out.

They hurried up the stairs as neighbors began to appear in doorways. They found Apt. 4, but the door was already open. A neighbor knelt on the living room floor beside a body; Gina's body. Kate stared at the older version that was definitely Gina. Blood ran down her face from the nasty bullet hole in her head, puddling on the gray rug.

Dair pulled a small, snub-nosed pistol from his coat pocket and pushed Kate back to toward the hallway. He advanced cautiously into the living room, glanced at Gina, then proceeded to the bedroom beyond. There he found Michael lying on the floor next to the bed, still clutching a wicked-looking knife.

He'd been shot twice, once in the leg and once in the back. Blood was pouring from both wounds onto the floor. Someone had wanted to make sure he was dead. However, he was still breathing, albeit shallowly.

"Quinn," Dair shouted, "get on the phone and get a couple of ambulances here."

He knew it was useless to tell Quinn to keep Kate out of the bedroom. She would knock him down and walk over his body to get to Michael. Sure enough, Kate was standing in the doorway, with a death grip on the door frame. There was virtually no color in her face and he feared she'd tumble to the floor in another minute.

"Is he…?" she started, stopped, then continued in a stronger voice, "Is he dead?"

"No, he's not," Dair answered while busily tearing sheets from the bed. "See if you can find some scissors or a sharp knife to cut this up. I need a tourniquet to stop the bleeding in his leg. I also need some pressure pads for his back, so fold some of the sheet for that."

Kate began a quick search and discovered Gina's sewing basket. She grabbed the shears and began to carve away at the heavy linen. She quickly fashioned a length for a tourniquet, then began furiously folding the lengths of the material into pads.

"Can you tell how badly he's injured?" she asked.

Dair felt for Michael's pulse, then said, "The bullet in the leg probably brought him down. The bullet in the back was to finish him off, but it must have just missed his heart. They probably thought he was dead, but he's a tough guy. Even so, he needs to get into surgery as quickly as possible. Where's Quinn?"

In response to his query, Quinn stuck his head around the door jam. "There are two ambulances on the way, Dair. I've also called the police. They are better prepared than we are to take statements from witnesses. And, I've asked for reinforcements here from the Paris head office. They've promised to send two more teams to assist. I can hear sirens now," he informed them after a pause.

Quinn added, "I'm sorry, Mrs. Evans, but Signorina Ghilberti is dead. Her neighbor said about 15 minutes ago, she heard the sound of running feet coming upstairs. That's unusual in this apartment building. Then she heard pounding on the door and shouts. She said she heard the signorina scream and a man say, 'Shut up, bitch'. Then there was more noise and three shots were fired.

"She said the noise going down the stairs was slower, like someone might be injured. She stayed in her room for a little while, afraid to come out to look. She's the one who screamed as we arrived," Quinn added.

"Why is this happening?" Kate asked with a slight quiver. "Why does someone want to hurt my family? I don't understand."

She was trying desperately to control her emotions. Someone had nearly killed her son; someone *had* killed poor, innocent Gina. Why?

Quinn had walked over to put an arm around her shoulders. He could feel her tremble through the knit sweater she still wore. He was desperately sorry that this had happened.

"I think it's time for you to call the American Embassy," Dair told Kate. "You need to let them know what's been going on. There needs to be a full-scale search now for the people who did this; and a reward offered for their capture. Also, you need to be safe. It's time to be Mrs. John Evans and insist on whatever action needs to be taken."

"I agree," Kate said, squaring her shoulders. "As soon as I get to the hospital, I'm going to call home and make sure Liz is all right. I'm also going to get the Evans Corporation's security office to send out guards for her and Jonathan until we know if she's also at risk. Then I'll call the embassy.

"Whoever is behind this, it's time for him to be nervous. I intend to bring all the influence I have to bear on this search. I want to find the person who let loose this reign of terror on my family. I want somebody to start paying for what they've done."

By now, ambulance personnel had entered the apartment and were stabilizing Michael to lift him onto a stretcher. Once downstairs, Kate said, "I'm going in the ambulance with him. Will you meet me at the hospital?"

Dair said they would and slammed the ambulance door behind her. He turned to Quinn.

"I sure as hell don't know what's going on here, but this situation just escalated bigtime. There's a difference between an amateurish kidnapping and murder. We need to start pumping every informer we've got. When we get to the hospital, will you let Giuseppe know what's happened. He needs to turn on his network. We need information."

CHAPTER 13

Intermezzo

The Vatican School
11 May 1975

In his private chapel, Monsignor Larosa concluded his prayers, crossed himself, and then eased back in his chair. For the past few minutes, he had sensed another presence in the room.

"Well," he said. "Report."

A large shadow detached itself from the doorway and bowed briefly before him.

"You were right to be suspicious, Reverend Father," the man said, "I believe Cardinal Messina's informant was deliberately misleading. I do not believe the Evans family has any idea that the Mussolini letter even exists.

"I have an invaluable source within the Evans' circle. He said the letter she holds pertains to the death of her husband. It is much more recent than the letter we seek. Interpol's focus seems to be on the missing paintings and the murder of the old priest. This has all just come to light with the arrival of the agents and the sharing of information.

Wasting any more time following them will not be helpful to our search."

"You're sure?" Larosa said. "We have only a little time left before this entire enterprise could explode. There's been too much bloodshed thanks to that black-market gang of thugs. They are obsessed with the money involved, but it's their disregard for life that has stirred this hornet's nest."

The man known as Orso, the Italian word for bear, was the primary fixer for the Vatican. He had worked closely with Monsignor Larosa for many years to solve delicate Vatican issues out of the public eye. The Vatican's own police department knew of his work, but even they left him alone and collaborated only when asked.

In spite of his size, he moved with stealth and grace through the backwaters of Rome. His network of informers, happy to give information to the Holy See, was unparalleled. Thanks to them, from the humble street cleaners to the valets of cardinals, he could quickly lay his hands on anything he sought.

His name was really Aldo, but his close friends called him Orso in his youth and the name had stuck. Together, they had built the network as they fought the Nazis.

He was also a master at thinking outside the box. His analytical capabilities would have made him welcome in any intelligence service. A phone call from his friend Giuseppe had alerted him to the change in the situation for the Evans family. He could answer truthfully.

"I know, Monsignor, and this morning they have raised the stakes again by attacking Michael Evans and his former nanny. The nanny is dead and he's in surgery. His mother and Interpol will burn Rome to the ground searching for the people who did this. The Evans Corporation controls too many enterprises around the world for them to be ignored.

"And, in the case of Alisdair Munro, his relationship to the legendary Angus Munro is well-known. Because of this joint pressure, someone, quite soon, is going to start talking," he said.

Larosa sighed, "Yes, and when that happens, we'd better know where to look for that damned letter and whatever it holds or you can add the Vatican to the list of innocent bystanders that will get burned."

"I believe I have information about that," Orso said. "I think what we seek has been removed from the box it once occupied and was made more portable. If we can contain the damage caused by our part in Mrs. Evans' kidnapping, I think we can bring our search to a successful conclusion."

"I hope you are right. Is there anything you can do to assist Interpol and Mrs. Evans? If not, then we can let them take care of that dangerous bunch of fools with their stolen artwork. We need to get all of these tangled threads snipped off once and for all," he said.

Orso slipped quietly from the room. He suspected he knew where Dair Munro was. One of his men had been following Mrs. Evans and knew of her trip to the Trastevere. Thanks to a message from Giuseppe, he also knew which hospital now housed her son. He was sure the other two were also at the hospital. It was time again to leave a message for Munro from the Blue Butterfly.

CHAPTER 14

Jealousy

Salvator Mundi International Hospital
11 May 1975

Kate sat in the surgical waiting room of the Salvator Mundi International Hospital, anxious for word on her son's condition.

She straightened her spine, then let her mind wander over the past. Hers had always been the role of strong central figure around which her family revolved. When Jack died, she'd had 24 hours to deal privately with her grief and shock; then she'd begun to minister to everyone else.

Now, however, all she wanted to do was curl up and hide from reality. It wouldn't do. Liz was frantic over what had happened. Michael was hanging on by a thread. The Ghilberti family couldn't begin to comprehend what had taken their Gina from them. Thank God she had Dair and Quinn beside her right now.

They had both appeared in the waiting room just as she was sitting down. It had taken nearly an hour to process Michael at this hospital that was renowned throughout Europe for its facilities and English-speaking staff.

By the time the paperwork was complete, Dair had come through the door. He brought her up to date on what steps they had taken to find Michael's attackers. Apparently, the investigating officer in charge of the case for the Rome Police Department was a Capitano Martini.

He, of course, had questions about what was happening. Dair had managed to fill him in while directing attention away from Kate for the time being.

They'd been waiting for the doctor for about two hours when the door opened and Ted Sanders walked in. Kate was flabbergasted.

"Ted, what are you doing here? How did you know where I was?" she asked.

"Liz called me when you were kidnapped, since you didn't bother to tell me," Ted said. "I was just landing in Rome when all this happened with Michael. I checked into the Hotel Cavalieri and they knew you were here. Apparently, Interpol informed them about the steps that would be taken for your security while you're in residence there."

He strode toward her, ignoring the other two men in the room and sat down. He took both her hands in his.

"Kate, dear, I can't believe you didn't let me know you were in trouble. I would have come immediately to help you. Now that I'm here, I hope I can take some of the burden from your shoulders so you can concentrate on Michael. I'm assuming that the security guard out in the hallway is meant to watch over you and Michael while you're here. That's good, but we'll get private guards for you as well."

When she could get a word in, Kate said, "Ted, slow down; it's okay. These two gentlemen are with Interpol. In fact, they are the ones who rescued me when I was kidnapped. They also were with me when we found Michael. They are cooperating with the Rome Police Department. So, it's not like I've been totally alone. Besides, you know I'm not, by any means, helpless."

Ted raised his eyes to meet Dair's as Kate was speaking. From the looks on both men's faces, they were not destined to be friends. Before anything more could be said, the doctor entered the room.

"Mrs. Evans?" he said. As Kate rose, he continued. "I am Dr. Moretti. I want to give you an update on your son."

Kate walked wordlessly toward him. She was steeling herself for bad news.

He continued, "The wounds are not as serious as we first thought. He has lost a good deal of blood, but the bullet which entered from the back was of small caliber. It did not expand in the body, but passed directly through after hitting a rib. That made it skitter off to the side instead of piercing the heart or one of the lungs. We've stopped the internal bleeding and tied off the affected blood vessels, so he will start to heal."

At this, Kate staggered slightly, then backed to her chair where Dair helped steady her. Without thinking, she grabbed for his hand and held on.

Dr. Moretti continued, "His leg wound was more serious. The bullet nicked an artery and if the tourniquet had not been applied as quickly as it was, he might have lost a fatal amount of blood. I'm happy to say, he will recover from both wounds. However, he will be weak for some time and will need considerable rehabilitation for his leg."

Tears of joy filled Kate's eyes and a slight chuckle escaped her. She explained by saying, "Michael was wounded in Viet Nam and spent a great deal of time in rehab. He's not a fan."

"That explains the scarring on his left shoulder," Dr. Moretti said. "He's very healthy and strong otherwise. I expect a complete recovery for him. He has been heavily sedated, so I suggest you go back to your hotel until tomorrow morning. He should be awake by then."

Dair said quickly, "Dr. Moretti, this attack on Mr. Evans was unexpected. We know that the perpetrators are still out there. Because of that, we would like Mr. Evans in a private room, as soon as possible, and we will provide round-the-clock security for him. I'm sure the hospital does not want the responsibility of keeping him safe."

"You are correct, Mr.?" Dr. Moretti left the name dangling.

"I'm Alisdair Munro and this is Quinn O'Malley. We are from Interpol and we are working with Capitano Martini and the Rome Police Department," Dair said. "We will have two other teams of agents also available to protect Mr. Evans as long as he needs to be hospitalized."

Dr. Moretti said, "All right. We'll keep him in the Recovery Room for another 12 hours. Then, if his signs are stable, we'll move him to a private room in our VIP suite. It is often used by politicians and movie actors who don't want their conditions broadcast. Our paparazzi are well-known for their dogged pursuit. After all, Rome gave them their name."

Kate asked to see Michael for a brief moment. The surgeon agreed, "Five minutes." Then, with a very professional smile and a quick pat on Kate's shoulder, the man was gone. Kate closed her eyes and sent up a heartfelt prayer, promising herself she would pray longer when she had more time. She opened her eyes and looked at Dair.

"After I see Michael, what's next? Do I need to talk to Capitano Martini or should I go to see the Ghilbertis?" she asked.

"I've taken care of Martini for the moment and I don't think there's anything you can do tonight to help the Ghilbertis. I think you've had a very hard day – again. How about finally getting to the hotel, a light dinner and an early bedtime with some sleeping pills if you've got them?" Dair said.

Ted immediately stepped forward and said, "Kate, I'll take you back to the hotel and see to it that you get what you need. I agree that rest is probably the best thing for you right now."

Dair added, "I'll stay here until I can get the security detail set up the way I want it. Quinn will be with you until you get to the suite. If you can get us an adjoining room, I'll take the first shift tonight as your security without needing to disturb you. Until this is settled, neither you nor Michael are going to be alone again."

"Thank you, Dair," Kate said gratefully. "I do need to sleep and then we can do some planning. Maybe by tomorrow, we'll have some word from Giuseppe's network about what happened today."

"The police looked at Michael's knife pretty closely. There is a lot of tissue, as well as blood on the blade. It looks like he really got one of them before he went down. That means someone may be looking for medical help, either at a hospital or from a private doctor. That kind of wound may be hard to explain. It might be the break we need," he said.

At this, Ted put a proprietary arm around Kate's shoulders and started to steer her to the door. Kate let him move her until she reached the doorway, then turned and said, "Thank you, Dair, for that tourniquet. You saved my son's life."

Then she turned and let Ted lead her away. Quinn followed them after sending Dair a wry grin and a thumbs-up signal.

Word of all this, of course, reached Milo Constantine. His informant in the hospital brought him up to date, so he didn't hesitate. He called a different number from his private list.

The next morning, two anonymous bodies were found floating in the river with their throats cut. They had botched their last job, and they would not be providing leads for anyone.

CHAPTER 15

Message

Hotel Cavalieri
11 May 1975

After checking into her hotel, Kate was able to secure accommodations with an adjoining door for Dair and Quinn. Although the hotel was fully booked at this time of year, Ted had managed to find a bed on the floor below hers before he came to the hospital.

After telling him she needed some time to herself before they talked, Kate left him at the elevator. The one small ray of light in this truly awful day was that her luggage was waiting for her when she entered her bedroom.

She stepped out of her clothes and into the shower. She let the jets of hot water beat over her neck, shoulders and face. This week was piling disaster on top of tragedy. Her darling boy had come within a hairsbreadth of dying. Her dear friend Gina was lying in a morgue somewhere, the victim of a senseless act.

There seemed to be no discernable reason for her or those she loved to be involved in whatever this was. She was currently clinging to the hope that Interpol and the police would be able to find some kind of motive for what happened to them.

She couldn't take Michael home right now, which is what she'd love to do. Leaving Italy and all the sadness she'd found here wouldn't necessarily mean she'd be leaving trouble behind. Knowing now what had probably happened to Jack, she was loath to run home. But dear Lord, she was tired.

After drying off and changing to warm fleece pants and a sweater, she looked longingly at her bed. She badly needed sleep and respite from her situation. However, there was still work to be done and no time to waste. If they were going to find the men behind this violence, they needed to get busy.

She moved determinedly into the living area and knocked on the door to the Interpol suite. Dair answered the door and she invited him in for a conference.

"What, if anything, can we do right now?" she asked.

"We are getting more agents here from Paris and we'll be putting together a round-the-clock rotation for protecting you," Dair said. "We also have the Rome police force guarding Michael with one man from Interpol on each shift with them. Capitano Martini is anxious to talk with you.

"The fact that you and I are involved in yet another violent attack in two days is not sitting well with him. The Carabinieri officer who was shot will live, but the old woman died on the way to the hospital. Martini is not overly impressed with Interpol. He doesn't like police agencies that cross borders into Rome."

"That's too bad," Kate said. "I don't want any trouble with the Italian authorities, but I have no intention of losing my Interpol bodyguards."

Dair looked at her and smiled, "Is that what we are? That's a lot of trust to put in people you've only known a couple of days. Not that we don't appreciate your confidence in us, but so far, Giuseppe has probably been more helpful than we have."

"You're forgetting that you two rescued the damsel in distress. And, you introduced me to the Contessa, who apparently holds Giuseppe's reins. So, I hope you'll stay with me as we work through this maze," she said. "I have to believe we are making someone nervous and that's good, I think."

"Could be, or maybe not. In any case, you and Michael are the strongest leads we've had in a while, so we will be sticking close," Dair agreed.

"I'm through letting others dictate the direction of our inquiries. That does not come naturally for me," Kate said. "From now on, I want to be on the offensive. Does that work for you? If necessary, I can have a plane load of Evans security men here in a few hours. You'd be in charge, so it's your call."

"Kate, I'm more than ready to be on the offensive," Dair said with a laugh. "And Quinn is always offensive. Let's go put our heads together and see what damage we can do. Then we can decide if we need outside help."

After bringing Quinn in, the three sat on soft arm chairs in front of the fireplace and Kate asked, "Do we know where all this started yet?"

"If you mean just with your family, it seems to have started with your husband's death five years ago. It's tied in some way with the missing paintings, but we don't know how as yet. Then things were quiet until you arrived. There was no assault on you in America, so it had to do with why you came to Italy and what you may or may not have found out," Dair said

"The real starting point seems to be the deaths of the San Sebastiano priest and housekeeper. However, the immediacy of your kidnapping would indicate it was also tied to the letter from the niece. You were planning to follow the same trail your husband did.

"You were also looking for Michael. And who knows where he's been and what he has discovered. Obviously, someone was trying to keep the two of you from getting together and sharing information," he concluded.

Kate said, "But I didn't have time to stir up any problems. Someone was waiting for me at the airport. Does that mean someone besides Interpol was watching me, even at home. They knew my travel plans and where I was going to stay."

"It's beginning to appear that your trip was practically broadcast to the world. Interpol knew; someone else knew to meet you at the airport. There may even have been a third party, as well, involved in your kidnapping. We've had a new wrinkle added to the mix that I haven't had time to tell you about yet," Dair said.

"Just as we were leaving the hospital, a nurse handed me a note. It was signed with just the drawing of a blue butterfly. I've had a couple of messages signed that way over the years and the information has always turned out to be spot-on for accuracy."

Dair handed her a pristine sheet of white, high-quality paper with a single fold. The carefully printed note read, "You should disregard the kidnapping of Mrs. Evans. It was done foolishly on the basis of erroneous information. Do not let it sidetrack you. A friend."

"Do you believe this? It seems impossible anyone would go to the trouble of kidnapping me because they had the wrong information. A woman died, for heaven's sake. What could that information possibly have been?" Kate asked.

"I don't know," Dair said, "but I do trust this source. And it would explain the strange way the whole thing was set up, with that house and the old woman.

"It seemed to be a very amateurish kidnapping. There was no ransom demand. In fact, no one ever heard from the kidnapper again. In any case, if we believe this, it leaves us free to move on to the more serious problem with Michael and Miss Ghilberti. There are no easy answers here. We just have to wait for Michael to wake up."

Kate shrugged. She wasn't hungry, but she knew they had missed another meal that day.

"Would you and Quinn like for me to order something from room service?" Kate asked. "I think I might be able to choke down a bowl of soup before we continue."

Dair took a long look at her and said, "If you'd like something, please order it for yourself. I'll take care of feeding Quinn and myself. After you've finished your soup, please take a couple of sleeping pills and go to bed. If you don't, your mind will race all night and Michael's going to need your brain rested and ready to go. I promise Quinn and I will be working late and we'll reconvene here in the morning."

Kate looked into Dair's grey eyes and saw the concern there. That, and his well-timed use of Michael's name, convinced her.

"Okay. I'll do it. Soup, pills and bed. I promise, though, that I'll be ready to go first thing tomorrow, so be prepared.

"I am going to add a phone call to the hospital to my program for tonight. I know they'd call if there was a problem, but I want to get an update. I'll also call room service and ask for carafes of coffee and juice to be brought up in case anyone needs anything during the night," she said

"Fine. Then we'll be right here for you. Once you're settled in your bedroom, either Quinn or I will be out here. I've already checked entrances from your terrace. You're high enough up that an intruder would need a helicopter to drop in, and we've got that covered. I promise; no interruptions tonight," he said.

As an afterthought, he offered, "If you'd like, I'll let Ted Sanders know you're closing up for the night and won't be available until tomorrow."

"Yes, I'd appreciate it. Give me an hour and then the place is all yours. That should give you a chance to get something to eat," Kate said as she walked to the phone.

The call to the hospital only elicited the information that Michael's condition was stable and he was still sleeping. Taking that as a plus, and with the knowledge that at least two guards were on duty, Kate ordered up seafood chowder. She managed to down about half of it, then took the sleeping aid she'd brought with her. Hopefully, tonight she'd get uninterrupted sleep and be ready tomorrow to tackle the maze of problems she'd found in Italy.

Good as her word, Kate had ordered room service for both suites. Dair saw the hotel had furnished bowls of fruit and platters of cheese and breads along with the drinks. The hotel had even tolerated his protection detail overseeing the food preparation. Someone had a bad habit of slipping Mickey Finns in the water. Fingers crossed; all would be quiet for the remaining night.

In the small hours of the morning, Michael surfaced from the blackness that surrounded him. He was conscious of pain. He was familiar with pain, but he was surprised to feel it again. Surely, he wasn't still in Viet Nam; that didn't feel right. Slowly he began to remember.

He'd been at Gina's house. They'd had a wonderful, if brief, reunion. Then his mother had called, excited that she'd finally found him. He was waiting for her when he'd answered the door. But, instead of Mom, two men had rushed into the living room with guns.

Gina had tried to help him, but someone had done something to her. Was she alright? Was she here? Where *was* here? Where was his mother? Did those men, whoever they were, have her, too? God, he hoped not.

If she was still free, he could count on her to pull out all the stops to find him. If Interpol was involved, as she'd said, his chances were even better. All he had to do was keep breathing. Then he drifted off again.

CHAPTER 16

Revelation

Back to the Hospital
12 May 1975

After an early breakfast, Kate, Dair and Quinn were once again trying to find a way through the quagmire this case had become. They were interrupted when Kate's phone rang with a call from the hospital. A nurse was letting Kate know Michael had regained consciousness and wanted to see her. She assured the nurse that they were on their way and would be with Michael in 20 minutes.

She didn't stop to alert Ted of their departure. Somehow, he had become a distraction she didn't need in her current search for answers. That was probably unkind of her since he'd so gallantly come to her aid, but her mind was completely taken up with the current situation. In fact, she wished he'd go home and take care of the Foundation. Had he left the deal he was brokering with the Met and the other museums up in the air to come here? Right now, she didn't care and wanted him gone.

When the three of them reached the hospital, they were immediately shown into Michael's hospital suite. The outer room was large enough to allow the two men guarding him to have a certain amount of comfort during their shifts. There were overstuffed chairs; lamps that could be dimmed; and coffee and water carafes.

Everyone stayed back as Kate entered the bedroom area to find Michael being examined by Dr. Moretti. She cast a silent question at the doctor and he smiled.

"He's doing very well for someone who was seriously injured just 24 hours ago. It's his youth and stamina that's standing him in good stead. However, I would like to limit your conversation to 30 minutes until he's had at least another day's rest. He'll tire easily," the doctor concluded.

Kate shook his hand and thanked the doctor as he left. Then she turned her attention to a heavily bandaged Michael and reached out to touch his brow. "My love, I'm not going to ask how you feel, but is there anything I can get you right now?" she asked.

"Mom, I'd really like a little water, but they are limiting my intake today. However, you can use these moist swabs to just roll around in my mouth," he answered, pointing to the cup on his bedside table.

Once she'd done that and delivered a light kiss to his forehead, she asked him if he felt up to talking. If he did, she wanted to bring in one of the Interpol agents just to listen. She beckoned to Dair, and he joined them, sitting unobtrusively in a corner while she sat by the bed, holding her son's hand.

Michael wondered if she even knew about Carlo. If she'd been busy looking for him yesterday, she might not. This was going to be a difficult conversation.

"Mom, I need to tell you something. It's going to be hard for you, but it's an important part of the story. Tio Carlo is dead," Michael said. "I arrived here Tuesday and didn't know where you were. I called Liz and she said you were in Rome. We both thought Tio Carlo would be at the airport to pick you up. So I went to his apartment that night and found him. He'd been badly beaten," Michael hesitated, then said, "and his throat was cut."

Kate's shoulders slumped as she digested this news. That's why someone else had been at the airport. Had the same people killed Carlo? This situation just continued to get worse. Carlo had been her friend and mainstay in so many of Jack's adventures. He wasn't that much older than she was, and he was gone. The violence sickened her.

She pulled herself together and said, "I cannot express how sad and how angry this news makes me. You know how I felt about Carlo. He was part of the family. Why? What had he done?"

"That's another part of the story I have to tell you. Three weeks ago, I was here to start a dig with him when I got word I needed to head for Viet Nam. I took one of the company's oil freighters. We managed to bring out 14 members of Danh's family before Saigon was overrun.

"But, before I left, Carlo insisted he needed to meet with me. He'd just found out some strange information about the church in San Sebastiano. You know, the one Dad worked on after the war. Apparently, that's where Dad was headed when he died. Carlo suspected Dad's death wasn't an accident. Dad was going to San Sebastiano because he'd gotten a letter from the niece of the old housekeeper there.

He paused to swallow painfully, then went on.

"The letter told Dad the housekeeper insisted the old priest he'd helped in San Sebastiano had been murdered, just as the war was ending. More than that, she recognized the person who did it. That's why Dad was hurrying to meet with the niece.

"Carlo and I agreed that as soon as I finished with Danh's family, I would come back and we would start looking into the accident. Carlo said he'd done some checking and the niece was dead now, too," Michael finished. The perspiration on his forehead showed how much the conversation was taxing his strength.

Kate gently swabbed his mouth again and said, "I'm glad you could help Danh, Michael, but I wish you had let me know. I could have told you that I knew about the letter. I found it when I was cleaning out Dad's desk; jammed in the back of a drawer. It's what started me on this trip.

"I can't wrap my head around the fact it also caused Carlo's death; but he was right. We now suspect that letter was responsible for your father's death. Who could have known he was going to see someone about Father Tucci? He didn't even tell me."

"I don't know, Mom, but there's a lot more. While I was in Viet Nam in 1973, I met Francois Benet, who ran the Beaux Arts School in Saigon. I went there one day to deliver an invitation and saw a painting on the wall. Mom, I was amazed. It had all the hallmarks of a painting by Van Gogh. It was done in brilliant yellows with a blue figure of an artist carrying an easel on his shoulder."

Kate stiffened as he described the painting. She'd taught her children well about the great European artists. If Michael thought it was a Van Gogh, it probably was. Was it part of the Nazi loot? "Did you ask the director about it?" Kate asked.

"You bet I did. You trained both Liz and me to recognize the good stuff. This painting glowed. Its quality was undeniable. I was told it had been donated in the 1950s by a young Vietnamese artist who trained in Paris before the war. I let it go because that's all he seemed to know.

"Anyway, the director told me to ask a planter named Pieter Van Hooten about it. I thought from his name and accent that he was Dutch. But, man, was I wrong. When I visited him in a cheap hotel in Saigon three weeks ago, he sat me down and he poured out this weird story. It turns out he was German and had been an officer named Hesse in the Nazi SS."

By now, Michael had two pairs of eyes firmly fixed on him. As the story continued, his mother and the Interpol agent were hanging on his every word.

"It was like he was waiting to tell someone and I showed up. He told me about a mission he'd been on in 1944. It seems he and an SS Colonel named Werner Lang had been sent on Hitler's orders to deliver a bunch of priceless paintings to a little church south of Naples.

"Apparently, these canvases were a bribe for Mussolini; to get him to stay in the war. There were about 20 paintings that were gathered in Paris, then smuggled south by Hesse. Those paintings were by Old Masters, mainly Italian or Flemish artists like Caravaggio and Raphael, but also Reuben, Botticelli, and Michelangelo. It boggled my mind."

Michael proceeded to give them the rest of the story, from storing the paintings in the crypt to killing the German crew. Kate and Dair were digesting the information as the rest of Michael's story unfolded.

"That's amazing, to say the least," Kate said. She knew he badly needed to rest, but couldn't resist asking, "Is there more?"

"Just a little," Michael said. "He thought Lang would kill him, too, when they got back to the coast, but he just told Hesse that he needed to go back to Paris to continue shipping out stuff on the trains. Lang was going back to Berlin to report on their success to Hitler.

"Hesse said he knew then that he needed to find a deep hole to hide in after the war. His Vietnamese artist friend had told him about the beauty of the country and the culture, which had been greatly impacted by French colonization. So, since he had no family left in Germany, he made plans to take some of the Impressionist paintings, those that were scheduled to be burned, as his retirement plan.

"And, that's what he did. He'd sold two of them in Switzerland after the war, using some of the dishonest French art brokers as middle men. He grudgingly admitted that the painting at the Beaux Arts was a real Van Gogh called *Painter on the Road to Tarascan.*" Michael paused, "And, Mom, he burned it when the Viet Cong got too close."

Kate was aghast to think that amazing painting had been so wantonly destroyed, but she quickly returned to Michael's tale.

"Lastly, he said he knew Werner Lang was still alive, and probably still working with an old smuggling ring he may have rounded up in Paris. He believed that Lang was still active in the black market and probably had something to do with the old priest's murder."

"This sounds like where our story begins," Dair said, stepping forward. "I work with Interpol and my name is Dair Munro. I really appreciate your information, Michael. I don't think we would ever have been able to connect all the dots on our own. Too much time has elapsed.

"If someone hadn't panicked when your dad came back, we'd be none the wiser. Jack Evans visited that priest in 1946, to help restore the church. He left about two months before the priest died. There would have been nothing to tie the priest's death to your dad's; especially at this late date."

Michael said, "Carlo was going to keep looking for answers while I was in Saigon. He wanted to find out how and when the niece died. He had a lot of contacts in Naples. Word must have leaked out to the wrong people. He sent a cablegram to me as our ship was approaching Manilla. He said he'd found some relatives of the old housekeeper and her niece in Rome.

"Not long before she died, the girl had confided in them. She gave them the information her aunt had given her about the killer. He wore an American Army uniform and called himself Captain Milo Constantine. Then the niece was killed in a hit and run accident. The car was never found, so the police closed the file. But Carlo thought he knew who that Army officer might have been from the girl's description. However, he didn't give me any clues in the cablegram."

Michael, running out of steam, paused once more.

"He was cautious, but obviously, someone found out about his suspicions regarding Milo Constantine. When I found him in his apartment, my very first thought was that they'd beaten him to find out if he'd shared the information. If I know Carlo, he told them to go to hell. So, they killed him. Apparently, anyone who gets close to Constantine gets killed. Please be careful, Mom," Michael begged as he neared exhaustion.

Kate was seething when they left Michael to get some badly needed sleep. Someone had nearly killed her baby and she was angry beyond words. Dair quickly filled Quinn in on events and stressed the importance of keeping Michael safe.

With the new information, they needed to reexamine the events of the past month. Once Michael regained his strength, he might recall more information. They were trailing a remorseless killer who'd had a lot of years to cover his tracks. Clearly, he had informants in the right places. They needed to be very careful who they trusted.

CHAPTER 17

Theories

Villa d'Este
12 May 1975

When Kate exited the hospital with Dair and Quinn, they sat in the car for a time, in silent contemplation of what they'd heard from Michael. Given the span of time over which the crimes were committed, it seemed unbelievable that no one had caught on sooner.

But one by one, all the witnesses had been eliminated and any relationship between the deaths had been cleverly erased. Why would law enforcement be looking for a common thread; a single mind behind it all? They wouldn't. In fact, they still weren't. It was possible no one would believe the threads they were pulling together. Most of the murders were listed as accidents.

"Do you want to go back to the hotel?" Dair finally asked Kate.

She thought for several moments, then said, "No, what I really want is to go back to the Villa d'Este and Bridget."

Dair smiled with understanding. The core of this problem was evil and black. The Contessa and the flower-filled villa were the direct opposite. He could understand why Kate wanted to reach out to his cousin.

Quinn continued to act as driver, threading his way through traffic until they'd once again reached the handsome gates of the Villa d'Este. As soon as they entered the house, the Contessa was fluttering around Kate, whisking her into the conservatory for a fortifying cup of tea. Only then did she ask about Michael.

"The doctor says he's going to be fine, eventually," Kate said. "He's lost a lot of blood and is going to need rehabilitation for his leg, but he will be whole again in a few months."

"I'm so glad for you, my dear. Once the doctor says he can be moved, you must bring him here. The hotel is very nice, but not as nice as my guest rooms. Besides, I have many idle members of my staff who will be delighted to spoil him. Giuseppe will see to that. It's been a long time since this old house has had a young man to coddle."

"You are so kind, Bridget. And, I think you're right. Much as I'd like to take him home and get away from all this drama, I know he'll be too weak for a couple of weeks, even lying down on our plane. They had to give him two pints of blood. His recovery is going to be lengthy. I've been through this before with him and I know he's going to get bored as he begins to feel stronger. You and your charming house will give him all the distraction he needs, I'm sure.

"Also, we're going to be very busy trying to find the man who caused all this. Knowing Michael is safe and in excellent hands will make it easier for me," Kate said.

"I'm so glad you're being reasonable, my dear," the Contessa said. "And I'm going to love being in the thick of all your planning. I'm sure you are going to need my help, sooner or later; mine and Giuseppe's," she concluded with a mischievous grin.

"Bridget, you're incorrigible," Kate said, with a smile, her first since they'd found Michael.

"Well, dear, I try," said the Contessa as she reached to refill Kate's cup.

Dair found them with their heads together sometime later. He and Quinn had been monitoring police progress on the shooting at the Ghilberti apartment, as well as putting together a timeline for the deaths they knew about as a result of Michael's added information. The aftereffects of the night the SS deposited the paintings in the church crypt in 1944 had really rippled through the decades.

Obviously, the colonel, Werner Lang, was one place to start, but like many former Nazis, he'd probably left Europe for a while, then returned with a new identity and a tidy fortune. Who was helping him and for how long? How many were involved? Surely, he'd picked up a number of associates by now? What was his game plan?

Dair couldn't shake the feeling that whatever Lang was doing, it didn't tie in with Kate's kidnapping. That fiasco had been too bungled for a tough operator who had gangs working for him.

Who kidnapped an extremely wealthy woman and had an 80-year-old grandmother as an accomplice? It made no sense. There had been no other guards around; none of the tough crew who had ruthlessly murdered Carlo Bernini and Gina Ghilberti.

Why did it seem like two different forces at work? And then there was the note from the Blue Butterfly. That source was always accurate; so apparently the kidnapping was a mistake. The mixing of the two events bothered him. Why it was done was a question he needed to set aside for now. Their focus should be on the known murders and how they were the tied to the paintings.

"I'm really afraid to ask what you two are planning," Dair asked as he entered the cheerful oasis that was the conservatory. Green plants and white rattan furniture filled the space, along with pots of honeysuckle and gardenia scattered around an indoor fountain. The tinkling sound of water made a peaceful backdrop to the women's conversation.

"Alisdair, my boy, do come join us," the Contessa said, waving him into a chair. "Kate and I were just discussing Michael. I'm going to have the pleasure of his company when he is released from the hospital. He'll add a touch of youth to this dusty old house."

Dair was thoughtful, then said. "I think that's a wonderful idea. We'll be able to shift all our guards to this house. I'm going to impose on you and ask if Kate can move in, as well. And, of course, Quinn and I. If we're all under one roof, it will be harder to pick us off individually. Ever since you got involved, I've worried about your being vulnerable. I know Giuseppe takes very good care of you and that you have state-of-the-art security, but having Interpol agents might serve to deter whoever is running this show; at least give him pause.

"I don't think his is a large operation if he's depending on a gang that he picked up in the 1940s. Maybe they have a few young guns, but I don't think there are more than four or five. If it was anything bigger, Interpol would have been tipped off in the past few years. It's hard to keep something like this hidden if it's too large. Unless they are Mafiosi, but I think this is either a German or an American operation."

"Why do you think Americans could be leading this?" Kate asked.

"It's a hunch, but the niece apparently told relatives that the guy who killed the old priest had on an American uniform. If he passed as an American, maybe he was," Dair said. "She'd have known if the guy had an Italian accent underlying his English."

Kate asked, "What have you been doing? Have you learned anything else while Bridget and I have been chatting?"

"Quinn and I have been trying to put together a timeline of events. Let's start with the first thing that happened. How did the thieves find out about the paintings in the crypt? Who knew about them, other than the Germans? Your husband didn't see any evidence of them when he visited the church, did he?" Dair said.

Kate shook her head. "No, he was there in 1945 and went back early in 1946 with a small crew and some church volunteers. But they never got any deeper at that time than the church floor. If there was a crypt down there, they never knew it nor did they open it. I'm sure," she said.

"Okay," he continued, "So, if he didn't know about the contents of the crypt, who did? We know Werner Lang knew about them. He wore an American uniform when he deposited them in the crypt. Did he put it back on to deflect anyone knowing he was German? Did he have time to go back before he went into hiding? Is he the man behind the black-market operation? Did he kill the priest because Father Tucci realized he wasn't an American?

"Did your husband take any other Americans with him when he went back in 1946 to inspect the damage and help repair it? If not, then how could any other American soldier know about the crypt? It was buried until late 1946, and by then most of the Army had gone home, certainly those in Italy. Even Jack Evans had left. Why would any of them be back in the little town that was still covered in ash?"

Kate said, "We may never know the answer to that. Would the timing have worked for Lang? If he was in South America or somewhere like that, would he have come back to Italy as early as that? It would have been very dangerous."

Dair said, "True, but if he had a good cover, he might have. Remember, according to Hesse, Lang spoke fluent English. I'm putting him at the head of the list because of that. I've checked. He was tried in absentia in Nuremberg in

1946 and found guilty of crimes against humanity. If he's ever found, the death sentence is still hanging over him."

The Contessa said, "Okay, he's our number one pick. If not him, though, who else could it have been?"

"Let's go back to the timeline. After the theft, the first crime we think we know about is the murder of Father Tucci. I think he probably died trying to protect the contents of the crypt. It was passed off as an accident. The reports say he fell down some stairs at the church.

"A few months later, the old housekeeper died as a result of a fall down the stairs at the rectory. I'd say that's a lot of accidental falls associated with San Sebastiano that year. Then it ends. But not before the housekeeper tells her niece about the American named Milo Constantine and how she thinks he killed Father Tucci."

He leaned over to fill a coffee cup and pick up a flaky sweet roll.

"Now 24 years go past and suddenly Jack Evans gets a letter from a woman claiming to be the niece of Father Tucci's housekeeper. She doesn't know about the paintings in the crypt, but she says the old woman told her the priest was murdered and gives his murderer a name. Furthermore, she thinks the same thing happened to her aunt. Why wait so long?

"We've been trying to find out if something happened in her life that spurred her to write to your husband. One of our analysts found an article in a Rome newspaper about his work with Fiat Motors in mid-June of 1970. The two corporations were going to form a consortium to fund repair works at Herculaneum and Pompei and build the long-delayed museum," Dair said.

He took a sip of hot coffee and then continued.

"Apparently, the niece, whose name was Francesca Leoni, remembered her aunt talking about a nice American officer named Jack Evans who came to help at the church after Vesuvius erupted. We got that from one of her cousins who remembered her talking about a letter she was going to write. The newspaper article included Evans Industries corporate address in New York and that's where she sent it."

"Yes," Kate agreed. "I remember that now. It was addressed to his office in New York, but I found it in the desk in Connecticut. He'd brought it home to keep it close. That's how he got involved with San Sebastiano again."

"That's at least a theory that holds water. Now, you said he didn't tell you about the letter. Did he tell anyone else? After his death, did anyone say anything about his going to Italy to see someone other than the people at Fiat?" Dair asked.

Kate shook her head, a frown line showing up as she concentrated on his timeline.

"When did she die?" Dair asked Quinn, who'd quietly entered the room and was listening to the discussion.

"Three weeks after that story came out," Quinn said. "She was hit crossing the street by a driver who didn't stop."

In the silence that followed, one could practically hear the wheels turning in their heads. With the information Michael had brought back from Viet Nam, they were getting very close to piecing the mystery together.

"Now here's the $64,000 question," Dair said. "If we think a lot of this was done somehow by Werner Lang, how in the world did he find out about the letter from Francesca? Once it was mailed, it would have been out of his reach. He couldn't have learned of the contents until it got to New York.

"Then it was in Jack Evans' hands, and he was very closed mouth about it. He wanted to find out if there was any truth to the accusation. He didn't even tell his wife or his son. So, who knew?"

"You don't think Lang had an informer at the Evans' corporate offices, do you?" Kate asked.

"Why would he have anyone planted there? His realm of activity was Europe. He might have known who Jack Evans was because of newspaper and television stories concerning his wealth or his philanthropies. I can't imagine he associated Jack Evans with San Sebastiano. He might have had someone here keeping track of the housekeeper's family," Dair said.

"Okay, let's go on," he said. "Things quiet down again for five years. There were no more deaths that we can attach to this timeline. Then things blow up again in 1975. Everyone and his brother seemed to know that Kate was coming to Rome, possibly because of the letter.

"She is attacked the moment her plane lands, and she's hauled off to that old farm. Even after she's found, the terror goes on. Carlo Bernini is killed the same day. The day after that, Michael is hunted by assassins who kill Miss Ghilberti and leave him for dead.”

They all sat quietly, digesting what Dair had said. Things began to form a pattern of sorts, but what did it mean?

“We have to assume it’s because of what Hesse told him in Viet Nam. He was given the story of how it all started and who the players were. He’s dangerous to them; thus, he must be eliminated. Most recently, we’ve been assured by a reliable source that Kate’s kidnapping had nothing to do with black-market activities.

“If we believe that, suddenly all the action shifts back to the guys who are killing, not kidnapping. All of this recent stuff revolves around this letter. Do you have it with you, Kate?”

“I think so. I put it in my purse with my passport. Just a second while I look,” she said, grabbing her handbag. As she shuffled through the papers from the zippered compartment of her bag, she came up empty.

“No, it’s gone. Who could have taken it?” she groaned.

“Probably half of Italy, considering it was handled by inspectors at the airport; the police when they were checking your belongings; or porters at the hotel as they were carrying in luggage. Even someone at the hospital. It wasn’t glued to you while you were getting Michael checked in.

“Most likely, though, it was taken by the man who kidnapped you. That letter might have been what he was after. I’m guessing that whoever took it turned it into a pile of ash,” Dair said.

"In any case, it's gone. However, if it was the letter the kidnapper was after, I'm betting this wasn't the one he wanted. That's why the note from my source said it was all a mistake based on misinformation.

"I've long suspected that our friend the Butterfly has close ties to another large organization in Italy, one that might surprise you. If I'm right, you were probably never in real danger, but I'm guessing our hapless kidnapper is in real trouble," he concluded.

"I don't care how much trouble he's in," Kate harrumphed. "I don't feel the least bit sorry for him. What I want to know is where we are on the timeline?"

"Where we are on the timeline is a very dangerous place, my dear Kate," Dair said. "There has been a direct line of murder and mayhem straight from those paintings to Michael's attempted murder. He survived. Maybe he'll continue to survive since he's told us everything he learned from Hesse. But all of us in this room are now in jeopardy since we all know many of one man's secrets. He's gone to extreme ends to protect his identity and his activities.

"We are close, much closer than anyone has ever been before. Moving in here together makes a lot of sense, but we need to be careful. Until we notify Capitano Martini of all our theories, our nemesis will be best served by eliminating all of us. Be warned."

Dair's words gave Kate pause. Her Irish great-grandmother supposedly had The Sight, the ability to see the future. Kate had never felt even a touch of that ability, but she certainly felt uncomfortable with thoughts of the coming days. Maybe her funny feeling was just good sense reasserting itself.

"Well," the Contessa said, "I, for one, am completely worn out after our trip down that ghastly timeline. I'm going to tell Cook to arrange a lovely luncheon, and then I'm sure Kate is going to want to drop in again on Michael. I think I'll go with her. Would you gentlemen be so kind as to accompany us?"

Count on the Contessa to brighten up a somber room. They all began moving around the conservatory, stretching stiff muscles and agreeing that lunch seemed like an excellent suggestion. Dair thought that the next strategy session would be even less pleasant than this one had been. The next move would hold danger for all of them.

CHAPTER 18

The Plan

Castel Malaggi
Later That Day

The palazzo of Umberto Malaggi did not originally belong to his family. They'd been small shoe manufacturers in Parma. He'd bought it from the heirs of a noble family following WWII.

He'd spent a fortune, most of it from dubious business transactions following the war, on the renovations and furnishings. He had no wife or children, so he was inordinately proud of the palazzo and anxious to show it off to one and all.

His parties were legendary for their over-the-top extremes in terms of décor, food and entertainment. As he lounged in his breakfast chair scanning the front page of *Il Giornale d'Italia*, he was interrupted by his butler, Luca.

"Signore, I regret to disturb your breakfast, but you have a call from Signore Milo Constantine," he said with great formality. It annoyed Luca no end that his current employer had no ancient noble title to toss around.

Malaggi was instantly on his feet. "I'll take it on the phone in the library."

The fact that Constantine was using his main house line and using his name for the servants meant this call would be more social than the last one. Settling himself at his desk, he picked up the elaborate gold receiver of his French-styled telephone.

"Pronto, Milo, so glad to hear from you. Are you in Rome?" he queried.

"Yes, Umberto, as a matter of fact I am, so I thought we should get together. A number of interesting things have arisen since we last spoke," the voice said. Its chilly tone made Malaggi shiver, even from a distance.

"Of course. Whatever is convenient for you. You tell me when you want to meet and I'll clear my schedule of everything," he responded.

"Good, very good. I have a few things to tend to this morning, but what about lunch at your villa? 12:30?" he said.

"I'm looking forward to it," Malaggi replied. "Arrivederci until then."

He waited for the click on the other end before returning the phone to its cradle. He never wanted that man to think he had hung up on him!

"Luca," he yelled. He had a bad habit of forgetting to use the bell system when he was upset. When Luca finally appeared from the bowels of the palazzo, he said, "Signore Constantine is coming to lunch. I want the chef to make something very special. I'll leave the menu up to him, but you must confer with him and choose the wines. Everything must be ready by 12:30 exactly. That man is always on time."

He patted at his forehead with his silk pocket handkerchief, realizing that his heart was racing. He was a 62-year-old multimillionaire and he was shaking like a leaf.

That man! I don't know why I ever agreed to go into business with him, he thought. I know we make boatloads of lira, and I get to keep the occasional masterpiece I covet, but working with him and his gang is not good for my nerves.

Abandoning the rest of his breakfast, he hurried down a hallway cluttered with statuary and artifacts he believed were all of museum quality.

When he reached an arched wooden doorway, he took a small, gold key from the pocket of his velvet smoking jacket. He turned the key in the newly installed security lock, then flipped on a light switch that illuminated stairs going down into a cavernous darkness.

Closing and latching the door behind him, he proceeded downward, flipping on more lights as he went along. Finally, he reached the bottom and turned on the last lights, which flooded the area with a luminous glow. Staring at him from the walls were the objects that he valued above all else. He saw eight paintings of incredible size and beauty; each in a special niche in this private gallery.

The first he came to was the *Inspiration of Matthew* by Caravaggio. This had been the one that originally seduced him. Milo Constantine had known his weakness for beauty and this had been an enticement he couldn't refuse.

As his eyes wandered further down the walls, he saw the *Cosimo d'Medici* portrait by Botticelli. By the harsh expression on that face, he wouldn't have lived long had d'Medici been alive to know what happened to this painting. But it was his now, and he'd earned it.

Across the space on the opposite wall was *Apollo & Juno* by Veronese; and it hung near Fra Angelico's *Last Judgement*. Canaletto was also represented by his masterpiece, *Piazza Santa Margherita*.

Although he wasn't Italian, Rembrandt had made the group with his *Annunciation to the Shepherds*. You just couldn't ignore perfection, he thought.

Reuben's painting of *Diana and Callisto* hung next to the last painting; the one that was his chief treasure to date. It was the long-lost depiction of *Leda and the Swan* by Michelangelo. It had disappeared sometime in the 16th century. Everyone thought it had been destroyed. He had no idea how or where Hitler's men had found it. Undoubtedly, it must have been in a private collection; hidden for centuries. Now it was his.

There were others, of course, who thought they owned the originals, but they had only copies. Two extremely talented artists had painted the copies for sale to gullible new owners. Each came with the proviso that the new owners were never to acknowledge owning them. If word got out about the paintings, they would be repossessed – forcibly.

Eager buyers knew this was no idle threat as Constantine's gang had recovered – very forcibly – one painting the buyer had foolishly bragged about owning. Umberto didn't wish to remember what happened to the owner. Others who had been offered the same arrangement had also heard about the dead billionaire, Constantine saw to that. The lesson was sufficient to assure no one else would be so unwise.

All of these masterpieces had been liberated by Milo Constantine at the end of the war. How had he come across them and how had he hidden them? Umberto didn't know – and didn't want to know. All he cared about was that they were now his. And, on very rare occasions, he was prepared to share them briefly with a few select friends or business associates of Constantine. That man's instincts were good, and he chose buyers who would abide by any conditions he set for the priceless art.

Constantine was careful to sell each painting to buyers from different continents. Only four copies of each of these were currently in other hands. But their new owners had been prepared to pay handsomely for paintings they could never acknowledge they owned. Umberto understood just how they felt.

Constantine thought it was about time to have another viewing party. Mixed in with his guests would be one or two potential buyers who had been carefully vetted. There was another Botticelli ready for sale, and the buyers wouldn't cavil at the seven-figure price when they saw it.

Umberto had been told that a special surprise awaited him if all went well. Constantine had been hinting for some time that there was a painting by Raphael that had been found; one that had been missing since the war. Umberto couldn't wait for the party and hoped that the luncheon today would produce a date for the next gathering.

While Umberto lunched with his associate, Dair, Bridget and Kate visited an improving Michael. When he dozed off again, Bridget headed to an engagement downtown and Dair and Kate returned to the hotel for a quiet meal. They walked into the hotel's private dining alcove, surrounded by ferns and fountains. A dolphin's-head fountain trickled behind them, providing a tranquil place to peruse the menu. Dair wanted to have a difficult conversation with Kate and he preferred a neutral battlefield.

"It feels good to just sit down and take a deep breath without worrying about potential catastrophe," Kate said. "That may sound a bit naive with all the upheaval we've dealt with, but for this single moment, I can be calm. I know Michael is recuperating under guard. I know Liz is fine because she's currently on a weekend trip with Jonathan. They are with 10 members of the rugby team he coaches.

"I think I know that the Contessa and Mr. O'Malley are all right at the villa. I'll just have to cross my fingers and hope that's true. And, I can see you across from me. Just for now, I'm going to try to relax."

"O'Malley was on guard at the villa last night, so I thought I'd give him a break and let him sleep late. He'll be hungry when he wakes up, but, he's always hungry. He ought to weigh 300 pounds," Dair said with a lop-sided grin.

Kate found herself thinking she liked that smile and it didn't show up very often. This man had only been part of her life for about three days, but those days had been filled with about six months of action. He was a very intriguing man.

"How long have you been working with Interpol?" she asked casually.

"I've worked with them on and off for about 20 years. It's been a kind of therapy that's also made me useful to other people," he said.

"Therapy, that's an odd name for such an active, dangerous job," Kate said dubiously. "I'd think a fortnight on the beach at Monaco might be more relaxing."

"Yes, well I wasn't actually looking for fun, more like distraction or a meaning for life," he said, suddenly more serious than she'd expected.

"I'm so sorry. I didn't mean to pry," she said.

"No, no," he said, "I'm sorry I gave you the impression you'd done something wrong. I don't talk about my reasons very often, although quite a few people already know. You see, I'd been a soldier for a number of years after the war. My Uncle Angus, whom the Contessa was talking about yesterday, was a legend in the art of warfare.

"He raised me from the time I was 12, and I'd become his second-in-command, even though I'd been too young to see much action during WWII. He was in great demand after the war to help train soldiers from a number of countries so they wouldn't get caught as unprepared as they had in 1939," he paused and Kate waited quietly.

"I saw action in Korea, but finally, we both decided I needed to get out of the military mindset and spread my wings. So, I went down to Oxford with Angus' approval to study arts and humanities. I met a wonderful woman who shared my interests and got married. Our little girl, Meggie, completed our lives.

"Ann, my wife, would take Meggie for walks in her pram every day because she was always eagerly looking around this big world. By eleven months old, she would point to things and try to talk to us. Anyway, I was blissfully happy. It was all such a change from my life before Oxford.

"One day, Ann and Meggie were coming to meet me for lunch. As they entered a crosswalk on High Street, a delivery van that was going too fast lost its brakes and plowed into them. They were both killed instantly, right in front of my eyes," Dair said quietly.

Kate found it hard to breathe. She could picture the idyllic family and the laughing baby. She could even hear the screech of failing brakes. Tears welled in her eyes as she looked at him; then she regained control.

She finally managed to say, "I don't know how you go on after something like that. I admire the fact you did and became what you are now."

"And what am I, exactly," he inquired with a wry smile.

"From my vast experience of the past few days, I'd say you are intelligent, empathic, and determined. You care about the cases you're working on and you care about the people involved. I, for one, was very impressed with how quickly you found and freed one kidnap victim – me – and how you saved my son's life," she said.

"Also, I was impressed by the way you started putting together the pieces of the puzzle as Michael was telling his story. I think there's a remarkable brain in there, in spite of pain from the recent loss of your uncle," she concluded.

"He was more than an uncle," he said warmly. "He was my friend and my father-figure. Everything I am today, I learned from him, by example or by experimenting. He was perfectly happy to let me fall on my face if it taught me something."

After a few seconds of silence, they finally looked at the menus and ordered.

Then Dair said, "Of course, he's gone now. He died so suddenly. I was unprepared; perhaps deliberately unprepared. I came to Rome immediately after the memorial service, but when we solve this case – and I promise we will – I'm going to have to give serious thought to my future; for me and the Clan Munro. Right now, how about a toast to the beautiful day and good company?" he said, lifting his water glass.

After a slight pause while their food was served, Kate asked, "Now that we have the broad outline of what got us to this place in time, what is our next move?"

"I think your next move is to take Michael as soon as he's fit to travel and go back to Connecticut. He's going to be vulnerable for some time and you've already been attacked once. It's too dangerous for either of you to get further involved. Your lives are too important to risk," he said seriously.

Kate looked up sharply from her salad and said, "Oh, I don't think it's going to be that easy to get rid of us. As you said, I've been attacked, tied up and otherwise threatened. Michael was almost killed. Poor Gina and dear Carlo were both murdered; as well as my husband.

"So, if you think I'm leaving with the question of who is behind all that still unknown, you've obviously not been paying attention to what makes me tick."

"I had a feeling you were going to be difficult," Dair said. "I know you want to continue this hunt, but you're both civilians. Word of your adventures has spilled out in certain quarters and your State Department is not happy with your involvement. Neither is Interpol."

Kate said, "Well, then, I suppose the logical thing for Michael and me to do is cut our ties with Interpol and go at this alone. Although, I know I could get help from Bridget and Giuseppe. We at least know who the players are now, or most of them. Carlo's death has made it impossible for us to just walk away.

"I am not your typical damsel in distress. I can bring in personnel from the company to assist us. And I know that Carlo has relatives who will be willing and able to work the streets of Rome for answers."

Dair threw up his hands in surrender.

"Okay, okay, I give up. I was told to try to dissuade you from continued participation in the case, but I knew you weren't going home. You need to call the American Embassy and let them know you have no intention of leaving. If they don't like it, they can take it up with some of the officials at home or in Rome."

"I can call Nancy Kissinger. She's a dear friend. She and Henry have been my dinner guests on more than one occasion. That should cover you as far as the State Department is concerned. Who would you like for me to call here in Rome or Paris or wherever?" Kate said, her cheeks still rosy from the flare of her temper.

"Never mind. When I tell Interpol you've cleared things with the State Department, I think they'll back off. You really are a dangerous woman, Mrs. Evans," he said.

"Remind me not to get on your bad side too often. They might find *me* floating in the Tiber."

"All right, now that we've established who is staying and who is going, what is our next move?" Kate asked.

"We know generally how this thing works, but we have no idea who the head man is. It may be Werner Lang, but it might be someone else entirely. I know a bit about Umberto Malaggi, and I don't think he's got the brains to head up something this big. He may, however, house some of the paintings. What we need is a look inside his palazzo to try to find some answers," he said

"What do you have in mind," Kate asked.

"I'm hoping Bridget may be able to finagle a way in for us," Dair said, with a trace of embarrassment.

Kate brightened visibly and said, "I think the Contessa d'Este has become one of my very favorite people. She thinks a lot like I do."

"Quite probably," Dair said. "And God help us all when you two put your heads together."

After spending some time in her suite talking with Liz in Connecticut and Nancy Kissinger in Washington, Kate joined Dair back in the car. They were once again negotiating mid-day traffic in Rome. On arriving at the villa's driveway, the gates swung open promptly when they buzzed. The front door was open before the car stopped.

"The Contessa will be with you shortly," Giuseppe greeted them, and on his closing syllables the Contessa hurried into the room.

"Oh, my dears, I'm so glad you've come back so soon. Kate, Michael is so nice and so good-looking. How have you kept the women from mobbing him up to now? I so look forward to both of you being in the villa very soon. Alisdair, can't you all move in now? she asked gaily.

"Well, we can talk about that. I wasn't sure how long Kate and Michael would be staying in Rome, but apparently, they are here for a while longer," Dair said.

"Oh dear. Did you actually try to get Kate to take Michael and go home, right when things are getting interesting?" the Contessa asked with a laugh. Noting Dair's disgruntled look, she shook her head.

"We do have lots to talk about. I've rung for tea. Would you like it here or in the conservatory?"

"Oh, Bridget, thank you. I feel we've done nothing but abuse your hospitality ever since we met," Kate said, "But since it's so lovely, why don't we eat in the conservatory so we can put our heads together about our next move?"

"Perfect, follow me," the Contessa said, whirling to lead her visitors through the house while unnecessarily instructing Giuseppe to notify Cook.

As they settled themselves under the glass dome, the Contessa said, "I'm so glad to see everyone looking refreshed after a few hours of rest. It must be all that strong Irish blood that runs in your veins, Kate."

"Hear, hear," Quinn added unexpectedly as he joined them. "Up the Irish, lass."

"My father would second that and order a pint of Guinness or a glass of Jamison's whiskey to celebrate," Kate said with a grin.

"So, Bridget dear, I'm sure you want to know if we have some sort of grand plan," Dair said.

"Alisdair, you know me well enough to guess I may be one step ahead of you when it comes to what happens next. But, please tell me your story while we enjoy this tea," she said, gesturing to the sumptuous feast of sandwiches, tea cakes, cookies and scones that Giuseppe rolled up to the table. Quinn looked especially happy at the arrival.

Dair told her of their theory that Malaggi probably had some of the missing artwork in his villa and that they hoped to get inside for a look.

"Yes, that old villa of his has a number of hidden nooks. I think the area downstairs, which is wired for electricity, and has heat, is probably your best bet. I saw it once when he was renovating it. And, with that in mind, I should tell you that he is giving a party this weekend for a select group of guests.

"You should send the Principessa d'Sforza a thank-you note. I believe she dropped a word in his ear about you, Alisdair, and your desire to see some of his new acquisitions. I might have planted the idea that I'd love to go and take a guest. She said she'd make sure Malaggi invited us," she finished with an impish smile.

"Contessa d'Este, you are a devilish old lady without a single scruple about getting your innocent friends in trouble," Dair said, waving a finger in her direction.

"Nope, not a single scruple. The party is Saturday night; at 7:30. I understand it's to be a costume party, which should make it easier for you to move around. And, I have every intention of attending, as well," she concluded.

CHAPTER 19

Betrayal

The past two days had been spent in hectic preparations. After consultation with the Contessa, Kate ordered costumes for the three members of their party. She had spent quite a bit of time fobbing off Ted Sanders, with only one afternoon spent browsing through the Galleria Borghese with him. She thought he had finally decided to return to New Haven to await their homecoming. She felt some guilt at being so remote with him, but she wanted to make it clear there was no chance of their becoming anything more than friends.

Fortunately, Roman stores were fully capable of providing elaborate costumes at any time of the year for fancy-dress parties. Therefore, she would go as Cleopatra with Dair dressed as Marc Antony. Quinn was also dressed as a Roman soldier, complete with spear and knife at his waist. However, their knives would all be genuine and sharp. The crested helmets were also equipped with hidden compartments that accommodated communication devices.

Kate's Cleopatra would be veiled and the soldiers' helmets had ear pieces that could anchor their masks without hindering vision.

Dair and Quinn were busy bringing in more Interpol agents and assigning them various tasks. Kate knew that he and Capitano Martini had been busy as well with the communication units, but she wasn't in on the details. When Saturday evening finally arrived, the plan had been for them all to go in one limousine.

However, upon arriving to pick up the Contessa, they saw that she had outdone and outshone them. She was Marie Antoinette, Hapsburg princess and queen of France, in all her panniered glory. With skirts that were fully four feet wide, she would need her own limo to keep from wrecking her costume. Dair rode in her car to help her exit without falling on her face.

As they ascended the stairs of Palazzo Malaggi, they found their host waiting at the door.

"Umberto, I'd like you to meet my godson, Alisdair Duncan Munro," the Contessa smiled. "And, of course, you may recognize Mrs. John Evans, chairman of the Evans Corporation and an avid art collector. I've been telling her about your beautiful treasures. I was sure you'd want to meet them and they are only in town for a few days, so I brought them along."

Faced with a *fait accompli*, Malaggi bowed and said graciously, "Delighted to meet you all. What a charming surprise, Contessa. Please feel free to browse the galleries. And do have some champagne, it's a special vintage."

As they passed slowly through gallery after gallery filled with paintings, object d'artes, and bibelots, each room began to look like the last one.

Dair said softly, "Bridget, if there is a private lower gallery in this building, where is the entrance?"

"I've given that a good deal of thought. I was only here for an hour or so during the renovation. The door to the staircase was an arched wooden affair of great age with heavy iron hinges."

"What do you remember about its location," Dair asked.

"It was quite far from the main entrance, closer to the kitchen area. The Principessa and I were just idly wandering around and came at it after we'd been upstairs. We came down an old servant's staircase, so I can't recall exactly," the Contessa said apologetically.

"I think we should split up to look for it, that way we can cover more ground. We aren't going to have much time before Malaggi comes looking for us. I'm sure he's suspicious about such a large party showing up unexpectedly," Dair said.

"Quinn, you head off to the right when we get to the next corridor, and I'll take the Contessa and Kate. You've got your communication mic and let's hope it works in this rabbit warren. Let me know if you run into problems."

Kate knew Dair and Capitano Martini had some sort of plan, but she wasn't sure of the details. Were his men listening to the communication equipment? Were police nearby if they got into trouble? She'd just have to trust Dair and hope their hunt for evidence wouldn't end up putting them all in danger. It was a little late in the day to start worrying about that.

As they went their separate ways, the Contessa took the lead toward the rear of the villa. They passed many wooden doors, but none had the look the Contessa remembered. As they advanced down one rather dark hallway, she stopped.

"I think that's it, Dair," she said, pointing about 10 feet to her right. When they reached the door. Dair tried the antique handle, and it wasn't locked. Still, the door wouldn't budge. Then he saw the newer brass lock nearly hidden behind the old iron. He pulled a lockpick set from his Roman breastplate, and bent over.

"The light here isn't great, but I have to do this by touch, anyway," Dair mumbled. After what seemed like an hour but was actually five minutes, he heard the tumblers release.

"Eureka, as our friends the Greeks would say," Dair said smugly. "Let's hope this doesn't squeal too loudly when I open it."

Slowly pulling back the heavy door, he was pleased to find a well-oiled and well-balanced mechanism. It swung open invitingly and they viewed a wide stairwell descending to dimmed light below.

Before entering, Dair sent a message to Quinn's headphone with the approximate location of the door. However, he chose not to wait for him and said, "I'm going down to check things out. You two stay here and wait for Quinn. This is getting more dangerous by the minute."

"If you think we're going to hang around in this drafty hallway where anyone can see us loitering, you are sadly mistaken," Kate said. "We'll go with you."

Dair knew he was fighting a losing battle when he looked at the Contessa and saw her expression mirrored Kate's. He shrugged, and took a step inside. There was a wall switch on the left that he flipped, hoping it wasn't attached to a silent alarm. Instant illumination showed the stairs were wide and steep.

He moved forward after reminding Kate to pull the door closed behind them. The Contessa had some difficulty managing her wide panniers, but they all made it safely down the stairs. There, they were greeted by an unbelievable scene. Lining the walls, in an echo of the best museum exhibits, were paintings of stunning magnificence.

As they moved forward, they were silent as they paid homage to the genius of long dead artists. Halfway down the aisle, they were startled by a voice.

"Contessa, I was just sure I'd find you here," Malaggi said. "I suspected the Principessa had told you of my private museum. In fact, I was planning to bring you all down here. I get to show it to so few people and I do like to share."

They all whirled to see him standing behind them with a smug expression. Taking a few steps forward, he gestured to the paintings.

"It's just overwhelming, isn't it? Just one of them would be the treasure of a lifetime, and I've got eight of them. Don't they make your senses swim, packed in here together."

Dair wasn't sure whether the man was joking or serious, but something made the hair on the back of his neck stand at attention. Malaggi didn't seem to be armed, but that didn't mean he wasn't dangerous.

"They truly are beyond words. How did you acquire all these?" Dair asked with interest.

"Ah, that's a very long story, and unfortunately, we don't have a long time," Malaggi said. "Do we?"

"No, we don't," a new voice sounded behind them, and Kate froze. She knew that voice, had known it for 30 years, but it couldn't be.

She slowly turned to see a staggering Quinn O'Malley being pushed into the chamber by a darkened shadow. Kate registered that he was missing his helmet, so that communication device was gone. He was bleeding from a cut on his head and seemed to be having a hard time keeping his balance.

Kate turned to the speaker and was momentarily confused. The caped red figure wore an elegant Devil costume, complete with horns and horrifying mask. As he peeled away the mask and close-fitting cap, she saw the familiar face. He was supposed to be on a plane to Connecticut, but here he was, armed with a nasty-looking Luger pistol. It was her dear friend and long-time employee, Ted Sanders.

"Ted! What are you doing here?" Kate asked in an unsteady voice. "You can't possibly be part of this."

She gestured at the walls and waited for him to tell her he was rescuing them from the demented Italian.

"But I am. In fact, Malaggi works for me. We knew how badly you all wanted to get into the palazzo, so we decided to have this party. You thought you were clever, but since I know so well how your mind works, Kate, I was always one step ahead of you. I've long wanted to tell you that good old Ted was also a criminal mastermind named Milo Constantine," Ted said with a smile.

"I've been leading a double life for 30 years, and it's been quite a nice life. Ever since my days with the Army, I've had all the money I ever wanted. And best of all, someone else has always been blamed for my activities; an old German, I believe. Why don't you all have a seat on the floor and we'll chat."

As they got down on the floor, the Contessa immediately ran into problems with her skirt. Malaggi thoughtfully brought a small bench over for her. They all faced Sanders as he continued his story.

"In 1945, I was working with the Monuments recovery people in Italy. I saw Jack a couple of times during that year. He and I had been together at the air strip in Italy when the old priest in San Sebastiano asked for him. When he came back to the airbase, he told me he'd promised to help during reconstruction of the church the next year.

"So, I guess it was natural for the old priest to call for help from Jack in 1946 when he found bodies in his crypt and the stash of paintings. But, fortunately for me, when the message came for Jack, he had just left for home. That was about the time he met you, dear Kate.

"I volunteered to go see what the priest had found. I was about to get my orders to go stateside, but I was curious."

He paced back and forth, yet never took his eyes off his audience, particularly the two men. He knew they were both dangerous and was staying well away from them.

"The roads were still a mess and the signposts were missing, so it was a hell of a drive. However, I persevered, and I'm glad I did. The church still had a yard or more of ash piled around the exterior, but the doors were open and workmen were coming in and out. The interior floors had been cleared. Father Tucci met me at the church and showed me to the crypt. He had kept everyone else away from it until the Army could get there," he explained cheerfully.

"There was no doubt about the bodies' uniforms; they were US Army. However, something seemed a little off. Later, I realized it was the boots. The Germans had borrowed the uniforms since they didn't need to fit exactly, but they'd kept their boots. Everyone lived in their boots during that war, and they'd better fit or you'd be in a lot of pain.

"Anyway, he had taken one of the paintings out of the container and spread it across a tombstone. Even in that dark, it glowed. It was *Painting of a Young Man* by Raphael. I'd seen it on a slide in one of my art classes and knew it on sight. I was seized by the strangest compulsion. I wanted it. Plain and simple, I wanted it and I was going to have it. In fact, I wanted them all and I hadn't even seen inside the others containers yet."

He stopped again, and said to Malaggi, "There's rope in the back hall. Please get it and tie their hands and feet. Make sure the knots are tight, and the hands behind the back. We have a couple of very slippery fellows in this bunch. We need to respect their talents."

As Malaggi followed his orders, Ted continued the story.

"I told the old priest that I would contact the proper authorities about the soldiers, but I wanted to clear out the valuable containers. I told him they needed to be shipped to Milan for identification and eventual return to their owners. I gave him my name and rank, Captain Milo Constantine. Then I hightailed it back to the base. I requisitioned a truck from one of the supply sergeants I knew well, and drove over.

"The priest took note of the US Army insignia on the truck and then he got some of his workmen to help me load the canisters. I told him I'd be in touch as soon as I could process them. I suggested he close up the crypt again to keep the evidence safe and tell people to leave it alone. I even gave him a receipt for the paintings, signed by Constantine.

"I'd mentioned the fact that my buddy Jack had been the one who came to see him earlier that year to help with rebuilding the church. I guess he'd liked Jack a lot, so he trusted anyone associated with him. He was so gullible; he bought the whole story. Then I drove off with a priceless load of loot. I hadn't even taken the time to look in the small metal box, but I did before I got back to the air strip. Man, I was totally knocked out. It was full of jeweled trinkets. The diamonds, rubies and emeralds just glittered on the pens, paperweights, and letter openers. It was like Aladdin's cave. There were also handfuls of loose stones of various sizes," he said.

He paused with a smile, as if remembering the feel of the stones as they poured through his fingers. Since no one commented, he continued.

"My sergeant in the supply office was, shall we say, flexible about regulations. He'd already 'liberated' several valuable souvenirs to take home. When I showed him a sizable diamond from the box, the avarice just danced in his eyes.

"I told him I had a load I wanted to take up to Switzerland, and needed some travel orders cut to that effect. He had contacts within the commander's office who would do that for loads he had to move for the Army. At this time, they were still supplying troops further north. In exchange for the orders, I was prepared to give him that diamond, and another just like it.

"I had my official orders that afternoon, and then I went to the commanding officer's office and told him I needed a pass to take a load of recovered items to Paris. I'd legitimately done that several times before; so, no problem. With the pass and orders in hand, that truck and I took off. It was a hell of a drive. I had to requisition gas a couple of times, and I had one flat tire that a bunch of GIs in France helped me change."

He was walking around, checking the knots as Malaggi tied them. When he stopped by Dair, their eyes met. He smiled at Dair's helpless position, then kicked him viciously over onto his side. He continued his tale.

"I crossed the border into Switzerland and headed for Bern. By now, I was on dangerous ground. I no longer had any justification for being in a neutral country. But there was a bank in Bern that we knew had been a Nazi hideout for stolen art.

"So, I ditched my uniform for civies from a farm clothesline and transferred the cannisters to a local truck I stole. All the time I was looking over my shoulder, waiting for the MPs to arrest me and take me to jail for about 20 years. However, nothing happened.

"I walked into the bank and told a bank officer I needed a bank vault for some large valuables I needed to store. When he saw what I had, he almost fainted, but he came through.

"They had several sealed areas that would accommodate the cannisters. When it came to terms, I was happy to accept his rates. I told him I'd want the area for at least 10 years. As a bonus, I offered him one of the smaller diamonds and a beautiful square-cut emerald. Needless to say, he agreed," he said.

By now, he was so caught up in his tale that he was strutting back and forth like a wind-up toy.

"Human greed is a wonderful thing. It has kept me in splendid style ever since my visit to Bern. As I walked out of that bank with the one and only key to my private vault, I couldn't believe I'd succeeded. I drove back to the farm; there still didn't seem to be anyone around. So, I swapped that truck for the Army transport, put on my uniform and drove all the way back to the airbase.

"The supply sergeant got his truck back, with a diamond bonus, and I left Italy the next week with the rest of the jeweled knickknacks hidden in my briefcase. Of course, I knew the supply sergeant had to go. Once he ran out of money from the gems I'd given him, he'd be back for more. He'd think I was an easy mark for blackmail. Just before I shipped home, he became another sad casualty of a road accident."

His audience had listened in stunned silence to his gleeful tone. As he turned a smiling face on them, proud of his initiative, he saw no recognition of his ingenuity.

Kate said angrily, "Is that when you started killing people who got in your way?"

"Oh no, he wasn't the first," he answered, "I had gotten away with my loot and I meant to keep it. That meant I had to deal with the priest. He was the type who'd keep calling the Army if he didn't get some quick answers about the bodies and the cannisters.

"I went out to see him the night I got back. I knocked on the rectory door and the housekeeper answered. She didn't know me from Adam; I just asked to see Father Tucci. When he came to the door, it was to see me as Milo Constantine. He invited me in, but I suggested we walk over to the church so I could examine the bodies again.

"He lit a couple of lanterns that were sitting near church door and he led the way again. As he leaned over to help open the crypt door, I hit him on the back of the head, catching him on that fatal spot the Army had so helpfully taught me.

"Then I arranged his body at the foot of stairs that went up to the belfry tower so that it looked like he'd fallen on those stairs, far away from the crypt. I ran back to the rectory and told the housekeeper that the Father had fallen in the church and needed an ambulance.

"That ended my association with San Sebastiano, or so I thought. I left the US Army to deal with the bodies in the crypt. Two days later I shipped home and back to civilian life, with a fortune in jewels that I sold singly to New York jewelers over the next 10 years, never using the same jeweler twice."

Kate again broke the silence. "But that wasn't the last time you killed, was it Ted?"

He hesitated for a moment, then said, "No, unfortunately it wasn't. I finally decided I would never be safe as long as the housekeeper was alive to identify me. A year later, I took a weekend trip to Italy. I found her in San Sebastiano, still at the rectory. I followed her one evening as she went home from church and dispatched her on the rectory stairs. No one ever connected it to the accident the priest had."

He added, "There were a few other fatalities along the way, but by then I'd connected with some Roman friends of an old Parisian gang I knew. They had collaborated with the

Nazis. I'd run into them while I was working with the MFAA boys after the war.

"For a handsome fee, they were willing to do most of the heavy lifting when we started the black-market business. Some competitors had to be removed. It was just business; nothing personal. It was lucrative for a time, but eventually the authorities got more interested us. I shut things down."

He finished checking the bonds on each of them and walked back to face them.

"Then I came up with the idea of selling copies of the paintings to less than honest buyers around the world. Because of my work with museums and the Kelly-Evans Foundation, I found that there were a number of well-heeled people who were greedy for beauty. They were not opposed to buying black-market art that could never be shown to anyone. In fact, it made the works even more desirable.

"I was able to use my underground contacts to find a couple of gifted forgers. Their work is close enough to the originals to fool those dilettantes who know nothing about art. I've had each of the 20 paintings copied four times. I make sure the sales are spread out geographically. The only painting that I haven't copied is the first one I fell in love with, the Raphael."

Kate finally interrupted this boastful recitation by saying, "I wasn't talking about any of that. I was talking about Jack. He was your friend."

"Yes, he included me with his friends," Ted said angrily. "They tolerated me because of Jack. I was his good deed. I wanted more. And I took it when the opportunity presented itself."

Dair watched as Kate processed what she'd heard. He knew the pain she was feeling at the betrayal. This man was a monster who'd fooled them all.

"And what about me, Ted?" Kate asked. "Was I part of the plan to take everything that was Jack's? Was I the last part of his life you wanted to own?"

Ted protested, "No, Kate, I wanted you from the first moment I saw you at your wedding to Jack. I spent years in hell watching the two of you build a family; shutting out the rest of the world.

"In my way, I loved Jack, too. If he'd left things alone, stayed away from that church in 1970, I'd never have harmed him. But he threatened my enterprise by digging into the situation at San Sebastiano. I couldn't let him find out and expose what I'd done. And he would have. Good old honorable Jack couldn't have let things alone. He'd have wanted justice for everyone. I couldn't be the sacrifice he'd make of me."

After a pause, he said, "Yes, that one was painful. He did set me up so that I could live a lifestyle that accounted for the wealth I had acquired. I was able to mix socially with all those blue-blooded jerks I'd met. I met a well-bred, acceptable wife and lived a gracious, boring life.

"But, my dear, she wasn't the wife I wanted. So, after Jack was gone, I took care of her; another tragic accident I engineered. This time in the pool, when I wasn't even around. However, I didn't know the old housekeeper had blabbed so much about me to her niece.

"Fortunately, Jack showed me the letter he'd received from her before he left for Italy. He asked my advice and I told him I thought he should go but not say anything to others until he was sure of something. Then I phoned my men and had them take care of his car. I didn't realize he left the letter behind, but you were nice enough to tell me, so no problem," he said coldly.

Malaggi shuddered, because that was the voice he'd heard so often over the telephone and during their occasional meetings. When Constantine used that voice, people usually died. This was not going to end well, and he wanted nothing to do with murder.

"You and Michael got involved and I did have a little trouble keeping my eyes on both of you. However, I could always keep track of you through the accounting department. I knew when you made your hotel reservations and I knew when Michael commandeered a company freighter and the company plane. In any case, Michael went haring off to Viet Nam after talking with Carlo, and Carlo started asking probing questions.

"Then you showed up with Interpol on your trail and got kidnapped. I'm still not sure who did that. Things were beginning to spiral out of my control. I don't like losing control," he said pettishly.

"Of course, good help is very hard to find. Those two idiots I had working for me bungled the job badly when I ordered them to question Bernini. I wanted information, not a dead body. Apparently, he'd been so uncooperative that they cut his throat out of sheer peevishness.

"After that, they sat out front to watch for people coming into the apartment and entirely missed Michael showing up. Fortunately, he left a message for you, Kate, at the hotel, that told me where he was. I'd sent enough paychecks to Gina Ghilberti to know her address. I knew the kids called her 'Tata', so his message was clear as day for me.

"But my men blew it for me when they left Michael alive. I knew if he lived, he'd tell you everything Hesse had told him. Oh yes, I had Michael followed from the ship and my man heard what Hesse told him. I knew with that background information; it wouldn't take you long to piece things together. After all, I was the only American military man left in that area in 1946 who also had access to the Evans Foundation and the donated paintings," he said while pacing the floor and shaking his head.

"You disappeared when you were kidnapped, but you managed to pop back up with the killing of that old woman at the farm house. The newspapers were very helpful in keeping me informed. When I knew you were with Interpol, I stopped worrying about you.

"I have a very good friend at Interpol headquarters in Paris. He kept me informed because his agents were dutifully reporting to him daily. Except, of course for this little gambit. I don't think you got permission to storm into this place without backup, did you, Alisdair?" he said with a sneer.

"After my men finished off Carlo to stop his questions, I decided it was time to tie up loose ends. I'll take care of Michael at the hospital while he sleeps. I promise he won't know a thing.

"Then I'll help Liz get over the pain of losing you both, and be so invaluable she'll want to appoint me chairman of the Evans Corporation. When I'm in control, I'll really be able to make my mark on the world. I'll step out of the shadows. Presidents and kings will beat a path to my door," he said, striking a pose in front of them.

"You just coldly killed your best friend, a priest, and your wife," Kate said. "You do know you're insane, don't you? Your time is running out. Someone is going to deal with you the way you dealt with Jack."

"Oh dear. Kate, I really do hate to tell you this. If there was any way to avoid it, I would make an exception in your case. But, unfortunately, all of you are going to have to die, in order for me to continue to exist.

"You see how it is, don't you? There's going to be a terrible accident and you're all going to be caught in a deadly fire that's going to start here in the hidden gallery," he concluded.

"What do you mean," Malaggi asked in a panic. "You can't start a fire down here. It would take hours to take down these paintings. They are permanently attached to the walls.

And any fire down here would spread to the upstairs. The damage would be immense."

"Yes, I know all that, Umberto, and I really am sorry to give you notice. I am cancelling our arrangement, permanently. You needn't worry about these paintings; they are all copies, too. You didn't really think I'd let you have my treasures for your walls, did you?" he said.

With that, he pointed his Luger at Malaggi and pulled the trigger. Malaggi still had an expression of shock as he fell. Whether it was because of the unexpected bullet or the knowledge that his beloved masterpieces were fakes, no one would ever know.

"Now, I'm not going to shoot you all. I don't want your bodies found riddled with bullet holes. So, I'm going to start a nice fire with some rags and petrol I brought down yesterday. As the paintings catch, that will add to the conflagration.

"If you are lucky, the smoke inhalation will kill you before the fire gets to you. But either way, the rope will burn and leave no trace. There will be universal sadness that all of you were caught down here when the fire began," he said as he began to walk past Kate.

She had been sitting with her back braced against an ancient pillar with her legs in front of her. It gave her stability and some control over her movements even though her wrists were tied behind her.

She had also been glancing toward the stairs occasionally, hoping for some sign that Capitano Martini knew they were in trouble. As Ted stopped to take his silly pose, she saw some movement in the direction of the staircase. She was sure it was a pair of black boots.

Everyone had been so engrossed in Ted's story; someone from upstairs had taken advantage of the lack of attention. Dair was on his side, his back to the stairs, so he couldn't see anything. As Ted approached, she decided it was up to her to create a distraction so that the boots could make their move. She pulled her legs toward her, then thrust them between his, causing him to stumble and almost fall.

He righted himself quickly, and snarled, "You bitch. I hope you don't die of the smoke. I hope you roast…," he said, stopping abruptly.

Behind his back, Capitano Martini and several of his men had burst into the light. Martini held a large machine pistol. As Ted turned to face this disturbance, Martini said, "Put down your weapon, now. You have no chance. Raise your hands or we'll fire."

Ted took only seconds to decide, then pulled the trigger of the Luger, starting a barrage that lasted just moments. His riddled body, blood streaming from several wounds, fell to the marble floor, only inches from where Kate lay.

His staring eyes were looking at her as he died. Good, Kate thought, he had finally been dealt with as he'd dealt with so many others. She knew that wherever he was, Jack was applauding.

CHAPTER 20

Safe

When their bonds were cut, Dair crossed to Kate and took her in his arms. She leaned her head against his shoulder and said, "I didn't think we'd get out of this without someone getting killed. I mean someone I care about."

"I know," Dair said quietly. "This is a lot for you to take in; it's a lot for all of us. I've been in some tight spots before, but this tops them all. Too many civilians at risk. I think I'm getting old."

He felt Kate nodding against his shoulder. He tightened his embrace, then let her go. Capitano Martini was examining Malaggi's body, then Sanders. "From what I heard over the microphone, Signore Munro, these two are the main players in the crimes we've been investigating," he said.

"Yes, I agree, Capitano. And I must tell you how grateful we all are for your prompt arrival. When we cooked up this scheme, I don't think either of us anticipated things going off the rails so suddenly. I'm glad you were able to hear what was going on, and come when you did."

"Yes, the transmission was a little garbled, but the extra antenna we wired into the Contessa's skirt projected much better than I'd hoped," said Martini.

"Wired skirt?" Kate said. "I didn't know about any of this. Was Bridget in on it as well?"

Dair shook his head. "We weren't sure anything would come of it. We didn't know if we'd even find the underground door, let alone get down here. And we certainly didn't have any idea we would be facing this, either. It could all have been a complete bust.

"I don't think either of us had any idea we'd catch all the big fish on the first try," he added. "You could have knocked me over with a feather when Sanders showed up.

"When he killed Malaggi, I realized we'd gotten in way over our heads. I never would have exposed you and Bridget to the danger if I'd suspected. I knew I could handle Malaggi, but Sanders was the killer. I think he developed a taste for it," he concluded.

"Yes, he certainly did like 'dealing' with people. I can't begin to tell you what my emotions were when he started telling his story. I was just filled with rage at the horrible things he'd done, but especially his callus murders of Jack, Carlo and Gina. I'd like to leave now," she said, turning away.

Dair rounded up the Contessa who wanted to go home to get out of the damned dress. "Alisdair, darling, I may be getting a little old for this much adventuring," she admitted as she got into her limo.

She leaned out and said, "Kate, since you don't want to come home with me tonight, please come over first thing tomorrow. We'll discuss moving you and Michael into the villa with a private nurse."

Dair promised he would bring her. Then he flagged their limo and his group settled in for the trip to the hotel. They'd promised Martini they'd be at the station tomorrow to give official statements.

As they pushed the elevator button to take them to the suites, Kate said, "I'm going to take a hot bath. I'll call room service and have them send up some drinks and snacks. Does anyone want anything heavier?" she inquired.

No one did, so as they entered her suite, Dair and Quinn turned toward their quarters while she headed for her bedroom. Quinn's head had already been treated by the hotel doctor. He was going to take a sedative and go to bed. She called room service, then proceeded to run a bath, using the lovely salts provided by the hotel to create a frothy foam of bubbles. Settling in, she began to feel her muscles release.

She'd never in her life felt as tense as she had tonight. She knew she'd come very close to dying. And, at the hands of a man she'd known and liked for decades! How had everyone misjudged him so badly. Even Jack, an extremely good judge of character, had accepted him as a friend and colleague. He'd paid for that with his life.

Reaction to the night's events was setting in and tears began to run down her face. She cried quietly for Jack and their lost future. She cried for Carlo and the friend he'd been to her through so many years. She cried for her dear Gina Ghilberti and the suffering her family had endured because of Ted.

Then she cried for the love her children had wasted on Uncle Ted. They would both be bitter; perhaps wondering if they could trust their own judgement of the people around them in the future.

He had made utter fools of them all; taking all he could get from them and leaving nothing but ashes in return. Before she could fall any further into depression, she sniffed and began to scrub vigorously at her arms and the back of her neck.

She worked her way down, carefully washing away the dirt and pain. Gingerly, she cleaned her ankles where the ropes had burned them again when she'd kicked at Ted. She needed to avoid being tied by the ankles for a while, she thought ruefully.

Ted had said he wasn't responsible for her kidnapping, but she couldn't imagine who else could be. Maybe his men had done it without his orders. She couldn't have made that many enemies in Italy. However, once the doctors gave their approval, she and Michael would move in with Bridget for a while.

When Michael had recuperated for a couple of weeks, she'd gather up her son and they'd go home. They needed to spend some time together with Liz. That would make them all feel better and hasten the healing they needed.

That left one glaring problem that she'd been pushing out of her mind for some time. What about Dair Munro? Yes, she said to her image in the mirror as she dried off her battered body. What about him? Her image didn't answer. No help there.

He was probably waiting in the living room to see how she was. In fact, she was certain of it. If she didn't make an appearance pretty soon, he would probably pick the lock on her bathroom door to see if she was all right. That almost made her smile as she slipped on her pajamas and warm cashmere robe.

"I've been making some plans while I soaked," she said to the waiting Dair as she entered the room. "I plan to give my statement to Capitano Martini tomorrow. I'm also going to move in with the Contessa; and I need to make a difficult telephone call to Liz. She's in for a shock, but I want her to know the nightmare is over.

"Right now, I'm going to sit for a while on my lovely balcony, look at the rooftops of Rome and try to relax before I go to bed. Mr. Munro, would you care to join me?" she asked with a smile.

Kate opened the French doors leading to the terrace and inhaled deeply. She could smell the pots of night-blooming jasmine scattered around the railing. She was standing near them as she heard Dair approach her with a goblet of wine in each hand.

"I brought red, but you can have white if you prefer," he said, offering her a choice.

"Red is fine," she said. Her fingers grazed his as she reached for the wine. Both of them could feel the slight tingle at the touch.

"Goodness," she said. "My wool robe must have created some static electricity."

He agreed quietly, "Undoubtedly that was it."

Somehow, she didn't think either of them believed that. Settling herself on one of the lounges, she reached for a nearby blanket to cover her legs. Dair was there before her and spread it gently over her.

Then he settled in the neighboring lounger and they stared out over the city as they sipped their wine. She could see the majestic dome of St. Peter's Basilica lighting the night sky. The lights of a still-busy Rome were spread like a carpet below her.

"What about you and Quinn? Are you headed back to Paris after we finish up with Capitano Martini tomorrow?" she inquired.

"No," he said. "I told you I'm not on the Interpol payroll as such. Neither is O'Malley. We serve on a contract basis. I think this week we've solved several longstanding inquiries; seven murders, for sure, and several others Sanders alluded to. Also, we know there's a mole at Interpol; somewhere high up in the command chain. It's going to take time to find that person and there will be some sweeping up to do, but we're not going to be involved with that.

"I'm going to take today as a great way to close out my career. I've already submitted my resignation. I need to go home now and try to pull together things that I've let slide since Angus died. I was only there long enough to bury him when I heard you were on the move. Now I know that you are safe and settled for a while, I can go back."

Kate was startled. "So, I was under surveillance for quite a while before we met?"

"Yes," he said shortly. "Remember, the Kelly-Evans Foundation was the only consistent clue we had about these missing paintings. It had to be someone high up in the company who was either handling the paintings or was being used by someone who had them.

"We needed to find the truth. When they found out you were coming to Rome, Interpol called me. At the time, we thought Sanders was just a cipher of no great importance. We couldn't have been more wrong."

"No," she said. "I was just the stooge and he was the man with the ideas. Sorry to disappoint everyone."

"Now, Kate," he said soothingly. "You know it only took me about five minutes to realize you knew nothing about what was going on. Unfortunately, by that time you had become involved because I'd told you everything. You were at risk then, and I didn't do a bang-up job of protecting you. You should never have been exposed to danger. I'll regret that for the rest of my life."

"You have known me for less than a week," she said softly. "How much importance could I have in your life after one week."

"Don't ask me that question if you don't want to hear the answer," Dair said. "We're both old enough to know second chances don't come around that often. We also know quite lot about each other after the stress we've been under."

Rapidly changing the subject, she said, "Why don't you tell me more about what you're going to be doing once you're back in Scotland."

Dair was quiet for a few moments, deciding how far to push the previous subject. Finally, he gave in and said, "Since I have no children, I need to find a successor. I'd like to have him beside me as I start pulling things together. There are several items that need to be addressed. Angus was ill for some months and problems that were minor, then, have gotten larger. I come from the northern-most Highlands of Scotland. There are forests that need thinning; croplands that need allocating; and sheep that need marking.

"I was gone most of the time for the past 15 years. I wasn't around to learn from Angus. Fortunately, his seneschal, or right-hand man, is still alive. He's aging, but he'll help me until I can stand on my own two feet. I'd like to have that young heir with me to learn at the same time.

"Being Laird of Munro isn't as big a deal as it was centuries ago, because we've lost a lot of the land. However, thanks to Angus and his penchant for picking up rewards for his service, being The Munro now includes another title. I'm now the Earl of Glenronin," he admitted quietly.

"I won't be calling the clan to war anytime soon, but our young men need to have training for careers or the clan won't have a future. Many of them, because of Angus, like to serve in the military. I have to ensure that they choose different branches of service. They can't all join up at the same time. Clans who did that soon regretted it.

"We have a loch that needs dredging in some areas and we have land that meets the coastline. Some of our families are fishermen and we have to have licenses and agreements for them.

"There are a lot of miles of highway within our boundaries, and I need to make sure the government keeps those in good shape. Transportation is a lifeline for our exports. I also have to attend our Scottish parliament when it's in session, or make sure I have a representative there keeping tabs on what's happening."

Kate was impressed. Basically, what Dair was explaining was the operation of a small, independent country that he headed. In addition, it appeared he also still had contracts with some countries to advise their military on arms and the training of their forces. This was a fulfillment of promises originally made by Angus Munro. How would he ever have time for a woman who lived across the ocean?

"Dair," Kate said. "It doesn't sound like there is much time left in your life for romance, certainly not with someone who doesn't live in Scotland."

"You'd be wrong," he said. "You wouldn't let me tell you how important you'd become to me in a week, but I'm going to say it anyway. You're the first one I think of in the morning and the last one I think of at night. That's not going to change when I leave tomorrow.

"There's nothing I can, or want, to do to change that. We're neither of us young anymore, but age does often bring the gift of wisdom. We don't have to wait for months to know whether an attraction is real or fleeting. And hormones aren't as likely to be the deciding factor. Although, I'll admit, mine have been engaged almost since I met you," he admitted wryly.

"I'm no fool," she countered. "I know something has developed between us this week. But my life is in Connecticut and yours, quite obviously, is in Scotland. We are both extremely busy people with others we care about in those places; holding us there. Nothing can come of this attraction."

Dair had noted that her voice saddened as she said these words. He took heart from that and said, "Things that seem insurmountable can be overcome if you just work together. The magic of air transport is a big help with that. And then there's that thing called the telephone. I'd even be willing to write a letter or two if that helps."

She removed the blanket and rose to her feet. He stood at the same time and reached for her. She moved willingly into his arms and he kissed her. A deep, loving kiss that filled a hole in her that she hadn't been aware she had. She moved into the kiss. He broke away, looked into her eyes, then put his lips on hers again. She sighed as she came up for air.

"Listen," he said, "I haven't told you, but I've promised to go to Yale in October to give a lecture on the reshaping of Europe from a military standpoint. There's a seminar to follow; then a big dinner sponsored by the St. Andrew's Society. I think there will be Hibernian games and music. I'll be there two or three days. Would you be willing to show me around while I'm there?"

She smiled as she slipped from his arms. "Why don't you send me an invitation? I'll have to check my calendar; maybe I'll have time."

She turned, went back to the bedroom and firmly closed the door.

The next day was taken up with statements, visiting Michael and moving in with the Contessa. That evening she drove Dair and Quinn to the airport. As they watched her drive away from the terminal, Quinn said, "Boyo, I can't believe you let her go like that. That's a once-in-a-lifetime woman who's driving away."

Dair just smiled. "October is only five months away. I believe she's going to do a lot of thinking. I'll be launching my campaign tomorrow. I plan to spend the summer wearing her down."

CHAPTER 21

Finale

The Vatican
Two days later

On Vatican Hill, the giant called Orso stood quietly in the shadows. He thought it was a silly name, but those he worked with in the Vatican thought it appropriate; and those on the streets of Rome feared it. However, he'd used the insignia of the blue butterfly, not a bear, on the occasions he'd contacted the Scottish agent at Interpol.

He'd been born with a perfectly ordinary Italian surname; as common as the English Smith or Jones. His family name was the only thing he carried with him in the aftermath of WWII. He guarded it like a rare and beautiful orchid.

As an orphan of that war's carnage, he'd been rescued by the Jesuit brotherhood and reared in their unyielding code in one of their institutions. There had been no motherly love, none of the softer emotions, so he had grown up without such things. He'd been unusually intelligent and that had marked him for special attention by the Jesuits. While love had never fallen within his purview, he did know about gratitude and duty. It gave him satisfaction to be of service to his brothers.

Tonight, he would be solving a problem that had nagged at the leaders of the Church for decades. Few had known of this threat; he had only recently learned of it. He could see, though, that the dread of it must have been almost intolerable.

A written confession by a Vatican doctor, the father of Mussolini's mistress, stating he'd administered a fatal dose of nitroglycerin to Pope Pius XI, would have been a catastrophe. To make it even worse was the admission that he'd been asked to do it by a Cardinal of the Church who was loyal to Mussolini. Real or a forgery, it had to be destroyed.

Now Smith was about to meet the man who claimed to have the letter. He'd spent time over the past decades hearing about the man he was about to meet. Strange that their paths had never crossed before, since they dealt in somewhat similar endeavors. However, he had always been on the side of the angels; while Lang was definitely a disciple of the devil.

He knew that Lang would be on his guard. He probably had some of his associates with him to act as guardians. He hadn't lived as long, and as dangerously, as he had without being very, very careful.

But the Jesuit's man was equally crafty. He knew he had offered an irresistible lure to reel in the old SS man. He was sure Lang would show up just to test the waters. He was to meet with him on the grounds of the Vatican. Lang probably thought that was safe.

As Lang approached the papal grounds, his senses were on full alert. He knew he was playing a dangerous game, but if he won, the rewards would be worth it. He had come in through the private east gate, and, as promised, he had not been challenged by the guards. He stood quietly near the famous Eagle Fountain, in the shadow of the tall monument.

There was a slight disturbance in the air, and he felt the tug of the leather garrot as it landed around his throat. There was pressure as the loop immediately tightened, but it was not yet lethal.

"Please stand very still, Colonel, I would not like an unintended movement to result in a nasty accident," Orso said softly.

Lang was surprised, but not terribly alarmed. He was here to negotiate and he felt he held the superior hand in this game.

"I appreciate the warning," he said affably. "Please don't do anything hasty."

"I believe you have something in your possession that my friends would like to obtain," Orso said.

"You will have to be more explicit," Lang said. "I'm afraid I have a number of interesting possessions."

The loop tightened ever so slightly.

"Please don't test my patience, Colonel. You know exactly what I mean. You have a letter that once rested in a box you left in a church in San Sebastiano."

"Ah, yes, that possession. I do have something like that," he acknowledged. "It's in a safe place."

Orso chuckled softly and said, "Yes, I'm sure it's safe. You move around a great deal while you are making your deals as the banker and the middle man for arms dealers and buyers.

"I wonder where a man would put something portable and precious as he moved from Egypt to Columbia to Taiwan at the drop of a hat. All the while, I might add, spreading the seeds of chaos and death."

Lang stiffened as he began to see the direction the conversation was headed.

"I'm just a businessman filling a need for my clients. I have no knowledge of what my clients do with the materials I provide. I assume they are defending themselves and their countries from enemies."

"Liar," came the rough response. "You are still Hitler's puppet; you've just gone into business for yourself. You are despicable. Wherever you go, people and countries die. You've dressed the SS in an Armani suit, but you still wear jackboots."

By now, Lang was deciding he'd made a serious error in thinking he could best any lackey the church could send against him. But he still held the trump card. He wouldn't be killed as long as he knew where the letter was; and they didn't.

"All right, let's stop fencing," he said. "I've got a dangerous confession signed by a prominent physician regarding a past pope. In exchange for the letter, you've promised a certain valuable consideration. So, are you authorized to finalize the business?"

"Oh, yes, I'm authorized," said Smith. He was tall, probably eight or nine inches over Lang's own six feet. That height gave him an advantage with the garrot and his long arms were attached to a torso that was pure muscle.

"I've decided that in order to keep the letter safe, you must keep it on your person. Am I right? Perhaps in a special pocket somewhere in your coat," Orso said, tugging a bit more on the garrot.

By now, it was becoming uncomfortable. Lang was tired of this game. It was time for his bodyguards to show up. He'd told them 10 minutes, and it had been that long.

"If you're expecting your team of killers to arrive, I'm afraid you're going to be disappointed. You were allowed an easy entry to the grounds, but your men have been intercepted and arrested. You are alone. Now, hand over the letter," Orso said, and tightened the loop perceptibly.

Lang knew he'd lost. His life was now on the line. He'd have to brazen it out and hope for the best.

"Okay, relax that damned cord a bit, I'm going to reach into my jacket breast pocket. I have to unbutton it to take out the paper. Please don't over-react as I move." He proceeded to do as he'd promised and lifted the envelope high so that Orso could see it.

"Please open it and hold it where I can see it," he ordered.

Lang opened the envelope flap and gingerly tugged out the letter. It was typewritten and very short. Smith pulled the garrot firmly while he drew a small flashlight from his pocket. He glanced at the letter and signature, then snapped off the light.

"That looks like the correct signature. Time will tell if its genuine," Orso said. "As a matter of curiosity, how did you obtain it after you left it in the crypt? You didn't get back there before Mr. Sanders and his crew emptied it."

"I didn't need to," Lang said. "I had the key to the box. I wanted to know what we were giving Mussolini that was so precious. The Reich's days were numbered and I knew that someday I might need an extra advantage. So, I extracted that bombshell confession from the box before we left the church. Since Mussolini never got there, no one ever knew."

"Very clever. You've always been clever, haven't you, Lang?" Orso said. "But this time, I think you've been outsmarted. Goodbye."

With that, he gave a ferocious two-handed pull on the leather garrot and broke the hyoid bone in Lang's throat. Within two minutes, Lang's thrashing stopped and he went limp. Orso then allowed the old SS man to drop to the ground like the piece of filth he was. He would get his cleaners in shortly to take care of the body. It wouldn't do for some late-night cleric, deep in meditation, to wander past and find him.

This was the second letter with ties to WWII to be discussed in Rome today, according to his friend, Giuseppe.

The other letter was part of the bribe's continuing saga. It had led Jack Evans to his death; and his wife, Kate, into danger.

That situation had also been settled. As far as he was aware, he was the only person left to know that there had been two master criminals and two letters. Both men were now dead. They had been so egotistical that neither had ever named a successor. The world would be a safer place without them.

An hour later, he presented himself to Monsignor Larosa.

"Did you find it?" the priest asked.

"Yes, Reverend Father, I did. I also carried out the sentence that the judges at Nuremberg gave Lang in absentia. He will bother us no longer," Orso said, handing him the letter.

Larossa unfolded the paper that had caused such consternation within the papal hierarchy and read the short text.

"Well," he said, "it's the right letter. Now whether there's a word of truth in it or not, I do not care. It was all long ago."

With that, he leaned forward and held the paper to the fire. As it ignited, curled, then fell away as ash, he gave a deep sigh.

"What did you offer him to get him to meet you?" the Jesuit asked curiously.

"Something he obviously coveted. I told him that if he gave up the letter, in gratitude, you would see to it that the

Holy Father made him an official resident of Vatican City," Orso said.

"As a bonus, his passport would have diplomatic status, so he could freely travel anywhere he wanted without hindrance. Given his activities as an arms dealer who traveled to many third world countries, it was a golden ticket as far as he was concerned."

Larosa laughed and said, "So he thought we'd hand him a get-of-out-jail pass from the Vatican. That's truly brilliant, my boy. It would have appealed to his vanity no end. But I can't believe he thought we would do such a thing."

"He has been operating unchecked for 30 years. He escaped his fate at the Nuremburg trials when he should have been executed along with the other war criminals. Instead, he has been wreaking havoc across the world with his trade in stolen weapons. I think he believed this was just the cherry on top of his ice cream – a bonus for being so smart in taking the letter 30 years ago. Besides, he thought I was just a negotiator. He did not understand who and what I am," Orso said emotionlessly.

There was a heavy silence as they stared at each other. Did the big man consider himself an avenging archangel, brandishing a flaming sword, Larosa wondered? It really didn't matter. As he sketched a sign of the cross in the air as a dismissal, Orso bowed and left the room.

Immediately, Larosa picked up his phone and, although it was late, he dialed the private phone number of Cardinal Messina. He knew full well the Cardinal was still awake.

After the connection was made, he said simply, "I burned the letter."

"Good," came the soft reply and the connection was broken.

EPILOGUE

New Haven, CT
21 October 1975

Kate Evans picked up the invitation one more time. She tapped it back and forth against the tips of her nails. It wasn't like her to be so ambivalent. She wanted to go, but she didn't. All of the adventures of the previous spring were fading into a comfortable past.

She now had two wonderful grandchildren, Liam and Bridget, and her darling Elizabeth had come through delivery with flying colors. Both Liz and Jonathan were holding up well with her occasional help and that of the night nurse who allowed them to get some rest after their busy days.

Watching Liz deal with her twins brought back memories of her own tiny newborns and how precious they had seemed, and miraculous. She was proud of how well they had both grown up.

Michael was now putting in more time managing his father's company, which allowed her more freedom than she'd had in years. She knew he wouldn't ever be satisfied just working in an office; no more than his father had been. To start with, he was still interested in locating the paintings

Ted Sanders had hidden away. That was likely to be a long hunt. But with competent advisors and managers, he could be out and about for extensive periods of time without the business flagging. He was extremely conscious of his duty to his employees and the corporation's limited number of stockholders.

When the invitation to the lecture had arrived, she'd put it aside, planning to decide as the date got closer. Well, the date was here, and she still hadn't decided. She'd known for a long time that he was coming. It was virtually the last thing he'd said when she drove him to the airport in Rome. She wondered if Quinn was coming with him. They had all gone through so much together.

There was no denying that there was something there between them. Both had loved and lost partners. Both had responsibilities to large numbers of people; his, the Clan Munro; hers, the Evans Corporation. While she was looking forward to backing off her long-time commitments, he was just beginning to get a handle on how to lead a clan of independent-minded Scots.

She'd spent a large portion of the past few months trying to sort out the damage Ted Sanders had done to the museums that the Foundation helped. Some of the art work had been reunited with the rightful heirs, but much of it was still residing in the museums. These institutions were waiting until some legal heir was found for the dead victim's treasure. For most of the recovered works, that wait would never produce such an heir.

In spite of the fact that he was constantly busy now, Dair found time to write. They were just quick notes, updating her on what was going on. He'd finished up the reports concerning the missing artwork for Interpol. Now he was back in Scotland full time.

That, of course, was one of the problems. If she were to allow things to get serious between them (always assuming they weren't already serious), she didn't think she wanted to live in Scotland. She had grandchildren now, and she wanted to watch them grow up. She didn't want to miss a day of it.

She also wondered if she was prepared to get into a passionate affair in her 50s. Menopause was behind her and she was feeling healthy, but it had been six years since she'd been intimate with Jack, and he had been her only lover. Would it just be weird to be with someone else?

Granted, she was attracted to Dair. She'd liked the feel of his arms around her; comforting after the things they'd gone through. She'd even liked (loved?) the feel of his lips after their one and only kiss.

Damn, I'm too old to begin again! She knew Dair wouldn't push her unduly, but he also wouldn't let her dither forever. He wanted her and he deserved a woman who wasn't waffling.

She suddenly realized that Hugh had come through the door and had been watching her for some moments. She'd never said too much about their adventures in Italy, but she thought Michael had filled in everyone about what had happened. She didn't know how much he'd said about Dair. Enough, apparently, to clue in Hugh.

"Would you like me to drive you somewhere this evening, ma'am?" he asked quietly. He'd seen the invitation for the past two months.

"No, thank you. If I go out, I'll just take a walk. It's the season that I love most on campus you know; crisp nights and gorgeous leaves," she said. "I haven't decided yet. I may just settle down with a good book."

He gave her another searching look, and she glanced away first. He knew and if he knew, so did her children. "I'll say good night then. Please call if you change your mind," he said and was gone.

Settle down with a good book! Is that the life she was looking forward to, after all the adventuring she'd done with Jack and the kids? She was still planning to travel and write, wasn't she? Her article and photo spread about the Contessa d'Este had been well-received. More offers were pouring in from magazine editors. Some were just looking to use her name and to boost circulation. Others genuinely wanted her work.

Suddenly, she wished she'd taken the time to talk more with Dair about his plans. Had he found the next-in-line for the title; someone whom he could train to follow him as laird? Was he planning to live in Scotland all the time? Was he going to do any more traveling; like this lecture tour he was on now?

Maybe finding out should be high on her to-do list. Grabbing her green plaid wool jacket and her keys, she left the coach house and circled the sprawling house in front to get to the sidewalk.

Turning toward campus, she allowed herself to walk at a brisk pace. Then, as she passed the University Club where she and Jack had hosted Yale's game-day luncheons, she slowed.

The lecture hall was just across the street. The area was well-lit and people were still hurrying toward the entrance.

As she stood across from the hall, still vacillating, she caught sight of Quinn. He waved to her and then walked unhurriedly in her direction.

"Well, looks like I lost my bet, Kathleen Mavourneen," he said with a mischievous grin and a thick Irish brogue.

Kate quirked an eyebrow and said, "What bet? And I'm not your darling, you big Mick."

"I told him you wouldn't come; that he'd let you get away when he didn't push harder in Rome. He just looked at me and smiled. He said you'd come. He said you wouldn't want to, but you would," Quinn concluded.

"Sounds like 'he said' a lot of things," Kate retorted. "Did he say anything about why he was so sure I'd come."

"Why don't you stay a while and ask him that yourself?" Quinn suggested as he put his arm across Kate's shoulders and led her, unresisting, toward the future.

Thank you for joining me on this adventure. I hope you enjoyed the book. If you did, please leave a review on the Amazon site where it's listed.

AKNOWLEDGEMENTS

I would be extremely remiss if I did not take this opportunity to say thank you to my team of Beta readers. They slogged through three drafts of this manuscript and were extremely encouraging. Without them, this book would still be laying in a drawer. They are Linda Carroll, Diana Malott, Mary Cameron and Carol Calano Sullivan. Amy Athey McDonald is the rudder who keeps me on the straight and narrow.

AUTHOR'S NOTES

A great many of the events in the book are true. Hitler did go to extreme lengths to keep Mussolini and his two million men in the war. In September, 1943, he sent a crack troop of paratroopers under the command of Captain Otto Skorzeny to rescue Mussolini from prison in the mountain hotel at Gran Sasso. Tired and in ill health, Mussolini wanted to retire. Hitler convinced him to stay. Who knows what he used as a bribe?

Mt. Vesuvius did erupt in 1944. It displaced people from nearby villages and almost destroyed the village of San Sebastiano al Vesuvio and the US airbase at Poggiomarino. Although the town was covered in ash, I seriously doubt any bodies of German soldiers were ever found in the crypt of San Sebastiano Martire.

Today, it is estimated that a path of molten lava one mile long, a quarter mile wide and eight feet deep rolled down the mountain. No wonder towns evacuated. Strangely, as I looked for references to this natural tragedy in fiction written about the war, I could find no other mention of it.

Pan American was the crème de la crème in international travel in the 1970s and their First-Class seat configuration was unlike anything seen since. The Hotel Cavalieri did and does exist on its hill overlooking Rome. The land belonging to Dair Munro, Glenronan, was my invention, but the Highlands of Scotland are as romantically beautiful as anywhere on earth.

As for my description of Angus Munro's service to the American Army, this was fact-based, but it wasn't Angus doing the training. Lt. Col. Thomas Hoult Trevor was the British commando who trained the US Army's volunteer ranger battalions in Scotland. They learned the seven ways to kill a man without making noise and other useful skills

So, what else is true? Jack Evans and Ted Sanders are my invention, but large numbers of the young men from blue-blooded Eastern families enlisted. They were usually officers and most survived the war. Shortly after his brother Jack received acclaim for rescuing the crew members of his sunken PT boat 109, Joe Kennedy volunteered to fly an experimental plane with a bomb that could be detonated by someone operating a remote control.

However, something went wrong and it went off prematurely, killing the crew. This paved the way for young Jack to carry the political mantle for the Kennedy family. Elliott Roosevelt did claim to have been in the chase plane, filming the action. Others said Elliott was just remembering what he had been told by a fellow pilot in his unit.

There was a fabulously successful group of art experts, originally formed by President Roosevelt in 1943, called the Monuments Men. These men (and women!) were originally two dozen museum directors, curators, art historians, artists, architects and educators. Their mission was to safeguard cultural treasures from war damage, sometimes in the face of strong opposition from US commanding officers.

The names of the paintings in Umberto Malaggi's dungeon are those of genuine, still missing paintings. It is painful to see the lengthy list of lost artworks. It includes not only modern Impressionist work, much of which was burned, but also work that had survived for hundreds of years when the Nazis got hold of it.

It wasn't until the 1970s that authorities began to put together extensive lists of still-missing works to circulate worldwide. So many absolutely priceless works were lost to the Allied bombing of Dresden and to the strange fire at the Friedrichs Hain Flak Tower in Berlin.

Hundreds of the most significant masterpieces in Europe were stored there for safekeeping and were burned in an accidental conflagration started by workmen. I was able to reclaim several of these for use in my story. Regretfully, none of them surfaced after the war, but I have given them new life for a short time.

Ernst Hanfstaengl, Putzi, was real. So were all the details of his life, except for his mentoring Werner Lang.

You may have wondered why I added the role Michael played in the last days of South Viet Nam. This story was set in the mid-1970s and Viet Nam was on everyone's radar then. This was especially true on college campuses where I was teaching journalism and working in PR. I realized that it fit chronologically, and I wanted to include a brief acknowledgement of the fact that those dying in the jungles of Viet Nam were the sons and daughters of the men and women who'd fought in WWII.

I remembered watching the television coverage of the last days in Saigon. Hordes of people who had worked with the Americans during the conflict banged on the gates of the US Embassy, desperate to escape. They knew reprisals would be deadly. While I was finishing this book, the same thing was happening again in Afghanistan.

Another genuine part of the story was a man I dearly loved, S/Sgt. Albert Francis Wilson. This grandson of Irish immigrants became part of the narrative. It would have tickled him no end. Sgt. Wilson became Al Wilson, the friendly neighborhood pharmacist who never talked about his war with his daughters. He was my father, a gentle man caught in a maelstrom of violence during WWII, who'd once asked me if I seriously thought I could make a living as a journalist. That was 60 years ago; and yes, I did.

He did not drive anyone around Italy because, after wading ashore on Normandy's Utah Beach in August of 1944, he was busy with his two water-cooled machine gun platoons. They marched, and occasionally rode, across France, Belgium, Germany and Czechoslovakia, as part of General George Patton's Third Army.

He did, however, use his gorgeous Irish tenor voice to sing with a GI choir after the war. They had been scheduled to go to London on tour when he was lucky enough to get his ticket home.

For helping me develop the idea of a second letter for the book, I give kudos to my wonderful daughter, Amy, a talented journalist who knows her way around the art world.

Having two letters and two different, but equally ruthless organizations to confuse the action gave the book more substance. The one Kate found in Jack's desk that brought her to Rome was the real cause of all the Evans family heartache. However, the second one, the one Colonel Lang held, was being eagerly sought by the Cardinal with as much desperation. So, two letters and two sets of antagonists; what more could you ask for?

Pope Pius XI was an aging man in ill health, and he was violently opposed to fascism and the oppression of minorities by the Nazis. He had, indeed, called the Italian bishops to a Congress in Rome to hear an encyclical he had others, outside the usual sphere of Church theologians, compile for him.

Many feared it would bring reprisals on the Church. He did die approximately twelve hours before he was to convene the meeting. At that point, the Vatican Secretary of State, Eugenio Pacelli, confiscated all 300 copies of the encyclical and destroyed them. He was named successor to Pius XI, and took the name Pope Pius XII.

Pius XI did have a doctor, Dr. Francesco Petacci, on the medical staff at the Vatican who was the father of Clara Petacci, Mussolini's mistress. That is fact. She died beside Mussolini in 1945. Did her father have anything to do with Pius XI's death? Was he killed at the order of Benito Mussolini? At least one Cardinal, Eugene Tisserant, wrote in his diary at the time that the Pope had been murdered. That claim was still being hotly debated in various periodicals as recently as 2021.

Pope Pius XI, was a rock star of sorts. If such a confessional letter from a doctor had existed in 1975, one that admitted there had been foul play, it would have shaken the Catholic world to its foundation. However, the letter confessing to his murder did not exist. It was a figment of my very active imagination.

www.ingramcontent.com/pod-product-compliance
Lightning Source LLC
Chambersburg PA
CBHW051813150726
47998CB00001B/141